NIGHTFALL

W9-BRX-412

NIGHTFALL

by David Goodis

Introduction by   Geoffrey O'Brien

A Black Lizard Book

Berkeley • 1987

Copyright © 1947 by David Goodis. Copyright renewed 1975.
Black Lizard Books edition published 1987. All rights reserved. For
information contact: Black Lizard Books, Creative Arts Book
Company, 833 Bancroft Way, Berkeley, CA 94710.

Typography by QuadraType.

Introduction copyright © 1987 by Geoffrey O'Brien.
ISBN 0-88739-029-3.
Library of Congress Catalog Card No. 86-71910

Printed in the United States of America

Introduction

David Goodis (1917-1967) has always been the mystery man of hardboiled fiction. Even his most ardent (mostly French) admirers had little but his name and dates to go on—while at the same time the savage content of his novels of low life and petty crime left plenty of room for imagination. Goodis was one of the most distinctive writers of paperback originals: a single-page of his work is instantly recognizable, as much for its prose style as for its characteristic obsessions. He wrote of winos and barroom piano players and small-time thieves in a vein of tortured lyricism all his own, whose very excesses seemed uniquely appropriate to the subject matter. As his titles announce—*Street of the Lost, Street of No Return, The Wounded and the Slain, Down There*—he was a poet of the losers, transforming swift cut-rate melodramas into traumatic visions of failed lives.

His own life, long hidden, has become a little clearer thanks to the French writer Philippe Garnier, whose recent biography of Goodis[1] (as yet untranslated) dredges up the secret corners of a life spent very much out of the public eye. As far as the world at large was concerned, Goodis pretty much fell through the cracks, and one's growing impression is that he wanted it that way. His career was not so much the *Retreat from Oblivion* that his first novel proclaimed as it was a voluntary and secretive descent into oblivion.

Yet clearly he was not without ambition. Born in Philadelphia, of a Jewish family struggling through the Depression on the fringes of the middle class, he apparently thought of himself as a writer from an early age. The first book appeared in 1938, the same year he graduated from Temple

---

[1]*Goodis: la vie en noir et blanc.* By Philippe Garnier. Editions du Seuil, 1984.

v

University—although going by the reviews it was no triumph: "The opening sentence of *Retreat from Oblivion* is as follows: 'After a while it gets so bad that you want to stop the whole business.' It refers to Herb's state of mind, but it's not an inaccurate summary of what one is inclined to say about David Goodis' novel." Rejected as a serious novelist, Goodis turned to the pulps, where he churned out endless aviation stories for magazines like *Battle Birds* and *Daredevil Aces*, and to radio, where he scripted *Hap Harrigan of the Airwaves*. His pulp writing, to judge by an early novella like "Red Wings for the Doomed," had little individuality; however, the experience unquestionably fostered the narrative craft which keeps his novels from dissolving into a morass of psychological analysis.

By 1946 Goodis was ready with another novel—*Dark Passage*—and this made considerably more of a splash. It remains one of his best-known books—the only one, in fact, that really made it into the mainstream. Today its appeal derives less from its none too believable plot (it was one of the early new-face-through-plastic-surgery stories) than from the author's obviously intense identification with his persecuted hero and from the jazzlike pulse of the prose. (Hero and heroine are drawn together in part by their taste for Count Basie.) With the sale of serial rights to the *Saturday Evening Post* and movie rights to Warner Brothers, Goodis had abruptly arrived. *Dark Passage* became a Bogart-Bacall vehicle and Goodis went on the Warners payroll as a staff writer.

He was barely 30, but his career had already peaked. *Dark Passage* was followed by another hardcover novel, *Behold This Woman*, a frequently ludicrous exercise in the *Leave Her to Heaven* "wicked woman" genre. The book is indispensable for its glimpses of Goodis' erotic obsessions, but it cannot have done much for his reputation as a writer. As for the screenwriting stint, all that came of it was an undistinguished remake of *The Letter* (Vincent Sherman's *The Unfaithful*) and an unproduced treatment which became his last hardcover novel (*Of Missing Persons*). He came close to interesting producer Jerry Wald in his concept for an epic film on "the entrance of our civilization into the atomic era": this was as grandiose a notion as Goodis was to be involved with. Henceforth his work would seek lower levels—much lower.

He had published one other novel during the Hollywood years, *Nightfall* (1947), a moderately successful thriller which in retrospect seems an almost perfect book, spare, balanced, and inexplicably moving. (The same might be said of the wonderful film Jacques Tourneur made of it a decade later.) The plot line—another innocent man on the run—could not be more routine. But in *Nightfall* Goodis creates an atmosphere where everything is symbolic—the oppressive heat of a summer night, a metal box of watercolors that crashes to the floor, the winding staircase where words of betrayal are overheard, the mountains toward which the hero flees—and at the same time densely literal.

Of Missing Persons, the banal police procedural salvaged from Warner Brothers, turned out to be his farewell to cloth covers. Goodis had no flair for writing about policemen or other authority figures. Only by identifying with criminals, derelicts, outcasts of some sort, could he come alive as a writer. His movie career was over by now too; indeed, his whole life evidently went into reverse gear. In 1950 he went back to Philadelphia (it isn't clear whether he quit Warners or was let go) and to his family: he would live with his parents until their deaths, shortly before his own. At this point he settled into ten years of paperback originals, mostly for Gold Medal books. There is no evidence that he had high artistic goals in mind. More likely he chose a kind of fiction which would support him while guaranteeing a cloak of anonymity. He doesn't seem to have wanted any sort of fame.

Garnier's account leaves no doubt as to Goodis' profound eccentricity. During the Hollywood years, for instance, he lived in the Los Angeles home of a lawyer friend, Allen Norkin, renting not a room but a tiny uncomfortable sofa for $4 a week—at a time when, as a movie writer, he could have lived well. Goodis apparently refused to spend money on almost anything: not out of miserliness but from a sheer perversity which also led him to drive the same battered Chrysler convertible virtually his whole adult life, a car so miserable that his friends refused to be seen in it. His clothing, as Norkin recounts, was equally grotesque: "He wore my old suits, and when they were really too worn out, he had them dyed blue. Finally his whole wardrobe was blue. . . . One day he invited me to eat at the Warner commissary. Dan Duryea was there, and Dave was wearing one of my white suits—which was all yellowed and stained. Duryea asked him where he had dug up the suit, and David replied coldly that he had bought it at Gordon's, one of the best tailors in Philadelphia. And when Duryea remarked that the suit wasn't even ironed, David gave him a pitying glance and explained that that was how it was meant to be worn. He also had an old bathrobe of mine. He went out at night in it. When he wore it he pretended to be a White Russian, an exiled prince of the blood." Goodis would borrow labels from his friends' finest clothes and laboriously sew them into his own wretched hand-me-downs, all for the peculiar pleasure of stopping people short when they criticized his clothing.

He also had a penchant for bizarre practical jokes like stuffing the red cellophane strips from Lucky Strike packs up his nostril, in order to simulate a nosebleed in the midst of a posh restaurant; or screaming with pain while pretending to be caught in a revolving door; or rolling down the steps of a movie theater as if the victim of an accident. But even more puzzling to Goodis' circle (which consisted mostly of old friends from Philadelphia) was his night life. According to what he told his friends, he preferred to spend his time in the sleaziest bars and nightclubs in the black ghettoes of Los Angeles and Philadelphia, in search of the most grossly obese women he could find. This obsession will ring a bell with readers of his novels, in which fat women play a major and often sinister role—nor are we too surprised to learn that what Goodis really craved from these women was extreme verbal abuse. In fact one is inclined to guess—given the overt masochism which continually surfaces in his books—that he went in for even harsher forms of abuse: but that is pure surmise. He was a man of fantasies, of masquerades. His night life—even the whole squalid world of his books—may have sprung largely from his imagination. Garnier even claims—astonishingly, considering the alcoholism of nearly all Goodis' protagonists—that the novelist himself was not a drinker. On the other hand Knox Burger, once Goodis' editor at Gold Medal, describes him as "a strange guy. He lived with his mother, in his forties, and would go off on these wild tears."

With the move to paperback originals, the style and content of his books changed radically. As if mirroring the failure of Goodis' higher-toned literary ambitions, the novels turned decisively toward the lower depths. From here on he would be the chronicler of skid row, and specifically of the man fallen from his social class: the disgraced airline pilot (*Cassidy's Girl*), the artist turned art appraiser for a gang of burglars (*Black Friday*), the famous crooner turned streetcorner bum (*Street of No Return*), the concert performer turned barroom piano player (*Down There*). In this fashion David Goodis, great literary artist turned streetcorner hack writer, could tell his own story and ply his trade at the same time.

Cassidy's Girl (1951) was the first and, judging from the number of reprints, the most popular of his paperbacks. It contains most of the elements of the later novels: an environment of grinding poverty, a sensitive but inarticulate male protagonist largely unaware of his self-destructive tendencies, and two women who divide his energies, with melodramatic consequences—one of them a frail ghostly alcoholic haunted by unrealizable dreams (let us call her Type A), the other a fat, rough-tongued, hard-drinking (and hard-fighting) woman who will stop at nothing to keep the hero to herself (Type B). There are many recurring relationships in Goodis' novels, but this polarity between two images of woman is always central; and the hero, caught up by his own lack of self-knowledge, is usually destroyed by it. He sees Type A as his true love, his only hope for happiness, from whom he is kept apart by Type B, who holds him in bondage through marriage, blackmail, or even the threat of physical force. What he can never admit is that he himself in some way sets up the no-win situation, and that indeed it is the Type B woman, that obese and muscular caricature of female dominance, that he really desires. Aside from establishing this tumultuous triad, *Cassidy's Girl* is notable for the schematic cruelty with which Goodis loads the dice against the hapless Cassidy. Disaster hangs around the fallen airline pilot like a magnetic, almost seductive aura.

The novels which followed—one or two a year for the next decade—were by no means all on the same level. *Street of the Lost* (1952), for instance, proves the most ham-handed of the Gold Medal books, emphasizing the prolonged fist-fights which were a Goodis sideline—he evidently had at least a fan's knowledge of boxing, and so his accounts have a somewhat pedantic precision—and the even more pro-longed drinking bouts which began to dominate his fiction. The next title, *Of Tender Sin* (1952), extending the alcoholic theme, resembles a poor man's *Lost Weekend:* Al Darby (one of Goodis' occasional white-collar heroes), tormented by the impotence which is destroying his marriage, embarks on an epic binge, revisiting the impoverished scenes of his youth, playing out a paranoid jealous fantasy almost to the point of committing murder, receiving wisdom from an old Negro on skid row (one of many philosophical bums to fol-low), and ultimately reawaking the repressed memory of an incestuous episode which is supposed to be the root of his troubles. Many of Goodis' novels follow a similar psy-choanalytic pattern; the thrust of his books is usually toward release, redemption, resolution of conflict, and there are even some theoretically "happy" endings; but whatever salvation Goodis as author may cook up for his characters, it never adds up to more than literary wishful thinking. The despair does not go away.

The Burglar (1953) was the first of three books that Goodis wrote for Lion, the enterprising paperback house which published the bulk of Jim Thompson's works. These were sharper-edged than the Gold Medal novels, with fewer uncontrolled descents into self-pity and (in two cases out of three) with more emphasis on crime. *The Burglar* stands out for its evocation of a Romantic death-wish in the context of low-grade crooks coming unraveled in the wake of a bun-gled break-in. The prose style is notable as well: Goodis seems to have really worked on this one, piling on little flourishes of syncopation that remind us how musical his ear could sometimes be. If Jack Kerouac had written crime novels they might have sounded a bit like this. *The Burglar* was later filmed by Paul Wendkos, a close friend who filmed on location in Philadelphia and hired Goodis himself to write the screenplay. It's in many ways an odd movie—

starting with the pairing of Dan Duryea and Jayne Mansfield as the doomed lovers—but a true evocation of Goodis' universe.

In its back cover blurb for *The Burglar*, Lion proclaimed: "Twenty years ago it was HAMMETT . . . for the first time telling the crime story with raw and savage truth . . . Ten years ago it was CHANDLER . . . taking the realism one step further—into the nightmare world of a murderer's mind . . . Today it is DAVID GOODIS . . . pushing the crime novel forward into a new dimension—probing into the heart of the thief and the killer." Whatever the accuracy of this as literary history, it pinpoints Goodis' originality quite well. The strength of his novels is the way his characters' emotions color every sentence, every line of dialogue, every fragment of physical description. It wouldn't be hard to imagine one of his books transformed into an opera—*Cassidy's Girl*, perhaps, as a swelling exercise in *verismo*. While at his worst Goodis merely overwrites, at his best he endows his icy streets and wretched shanties with expressionistic intensity.

The central law of Goodis' fiction is that happiness is forbidden. All true love remains unconsummated; all petty criminals (a breed with whom the author closely identifies) are caught ignominiously; all proud old men are humiliated; all virgins are molested. The sentimental lyricism of Goodis' prose masks a savage perception of life. In *The Moon in the Gutter* (1953), a dockworker's sister is raped; she slits her throat with a razor in a garbage-strewn alleyway. Later in the book, a slumming socialite trying to seduce the dockworker drives him over to the harbor, saying "It's really magnificent." He replies with a nauseating description of the smell and texture of bilgewater, and when she recoils adds: "I'm only trying to give you the full picture. You come down to see the dirt, I'm showing you the dirt." In a memorably overblown final monologue, he indicts the moon shining above the gutter for his sister's death.

Goodis published three novels in 1954, two of them among his best. Gold Medal's *Street of No Return* almost ranks as an epic: a wino's odyssey from nowhere to nowhere. Three bums stand on a corner trying to figure out how to get a drink. One of them wanders off and comes back 175 pages later, a bottle under his coat, having relived his entire life: his career as a pop singer shattered by an obsessive love for a prostitute, his torture by racketeers and his beating at the hands of the police, his final turn as a reluctant hero foiling a conspiracy to foment a race riot—only to find that all he really wants to do is go back to the corner. Here Goodis came closest to acknowledging that his heroes' tragic destinies were largely self-created. His battered protagonist finally admits to himself: "You've played a losing game and actually enjoyed the idea of losing, almost like them freaks who get their kicks when they're banged around. . . . You're in that same bracket, buddy. You're one of them less-than-nothings who like the taste of being hurt." He moves inevitably toward the numbed retreat of the book's final sentence: "They sat there passing the bottle around, and there was nothing that could bother them, nothing at all."

In a similar spirit, the artist hero of *Black Friday*, having witnessed the violent collapse of the gang of burglars he had joined and the self-sacrificing death of the pale girl he loved, walks off into the night: "He had no idea where he was going and he didn't care." A more elaborate variation on the themes of *The Burglar*, *Black Friday* shows Goodis at a peak of tonal control. His sense of the criminal band as a world apart, with its own hermetic codes of respect and kinship, informs every action in the book from first to last. Outside the law there is no freedom, only a stifling web of compulsions and obligations.

A key to all this inner turmoil can be found in *The Blonde on the Street Corner*, a period piece set in the 1930s and which has all the earmarks of an autobiographical novel. (Apparently it has some connection with his unfilmed scenario about the atomic era.) The young hero, whose family struggles, like Goodis', with the adversities of the Depression, is an aspiring songwriter still buoyed by the optimism of youth. The novel is essentially the story of how his hopes are nipped in the bud as he yields to the aggressive advances of the blonde of the title, a violent, alcoholic older woman who brings him face to face with his real sexual nature. This work stands alone in the Goodis *oeuvre*, and is by the way another example of Lion Books' remarkable openness to the offbeat.

The remaining books can be dealt with more cursorily. *The Wounded and the Slain* (1955) offers us another white-collar drunk, on vacation in Jamaica with his frigid wife and doing his best to get himself killed in barroom brawls. This is Goodis' most thorough dissection of alcoholism, but the book rapidly loses credibility as the hero becomes accidentally involved with the Kingston underworld and ends by triumphing over his problems in a clumsily arranged denouement. Far more successful is *Down There* (1956), best known as the source of Francois Truffaut's *Shoot the Piano Player*. Here Goodis blends two of his favorite themes—the artist on the skids and the criminal gang as surrogate family (in this case the gang *is* a family)—to produce his last really satisfying novel. (*Down There* might be seen as the last panel of a triptych also encompassing *The Burglar* and *Black Friday*.)

The next book, *Fire in the Flesh* (1957), purveys the unlikely tale of a pyromaniac who discovers that the only way he can control his impulses is to immerse himself in cheap wine. In a final catharsis he realizes the roots of his obsession and is cured. *Night Squad* (1961), another minor effort, concerns a crooked cop turned alcoholic who likewise finds redemption at the eleventh hour. Goodis' last novel, the posthumously published *Somebody's Done For* (1967), amounts to a pot-pourri of his major preoccupations—the two women, the gang as family, alcoholism, impotence, incest—played out on a barren strip of New Jersey shoreline. These final works, presumably reflecting the author's state of mind, are suffused with a depression that creeps into the rhythm of the sentences.

From about midway in his career Goodis shows every sign of having reached a personal impasse. The obsessions laid bare in his novels begin to repeat themselves rather than developing creatively. But taken as a whole his writing represents an astonishing example of self-revelation in the context of genre fiction. Anyone who spends some time with his books learns to identify their peculiarly intense atmosphere, their outbursts of eloquence, their sense of the world as an abyss made for falling into. That such testaments of deprivation and anxiety could have sustained a career as a paperback novelist is today cause for wonderment. Nothing so downbeat, so wedded to reiterations of personal and social failure, would be likely to find a mass market publisher at present. The absolutely personal voice of David Goodis seems almost to have escaped by accident. It emanated from the heart of an efficient entertainment industry, startlingly, like the wailing of an outcast.

Geoffrey O'Brien

Geoffrey O'Brien is the author of *Hardboiled America: The Lurid Years of Paperbacks*.

Chapter One

It was one of those hot sticky nights that makes Manhattan show its age. There was something dreary and stagnant in the way all this syrupy beat refused to budge. It was anything but a night for labor, and Vanning stood up and walked away from the tilted drawing board. He brushed past a large metal box of water colors, heard the crash as the box hit the floor. That seemed to do it. That ended any inclination he might have had for finishing the job tonight.

Heat came into the room and settled itself on Vanning. He lit a cigarette. He told himself it was time for another drink. Walking to the window, he told himself to get away from the idea of liquor. The heat was stronger than liquor.

He stood there at the window, looking out upon Greenwich Village, seeing the lights, hearing noises in the streets. He had a desire to be part of the noise. He wanted to get some of those lights, wanted to get in on that activity out there, whatever it was. He wanted to talk to somebody. He wanted to go out.

He was afraid to go out.

And he realized that. The realization brought on more fright. He rubbed his hands into his eyes and wondered what was making this night such a difficult thing. And suddenly he was telling himself that something was going to happen tonight.

It was more than a premonition. There was considerable reason for making the forecast. It had nothing to do with the night itself. It was a process of going back, and with his eyes closed he could see a progression of scenes that made him shiver without moving, swallow hard without swallowing anything.

There was a pale blue automobile, a convertible. That was a logical color, that pale blue, logical for the start of it, because it had started out in a pale, quiet way, the pale blue

1

convertible cruising along peacefully, the Colorado mountainside so calm and pretty, the sky so contented, all of this scene pale blue in a nice even sort of style. And then red came into it, glaring red, the hood and fenders of the smashed station wagon, the hard gray of the boulder against which the wrecked car was resting, the hard gray turning into black, the black of the revolver, the black remaining as more colors moved in. The green of the hotel room, the orange carpet, or maybe it wasn't orange—it could have been purple, a lot of those colors could have been other colors—but the one color about which there was no mistake was black. Because black was the color of a gun, a dull black, a complete black, and through a whirl of all the colors coming together in a pool gone wild, the black gun came into his hand and he held it there for a time impossible to measure, and then he pointed the black gun and he pulled the trigger and he killed a man.

He took his clenched fists away from his eyes, opened his eyes and brought himself back to this room. Turning, he saw the drawing board, and it threw an invisible rope toward him, the rope pulling him in, urging him to get away from yesterday and stay with now. Because now had him listed as james Vanning, a commercial artist specializing in the more intricate kind of work that art departments of advertising agencies hand out to proven experts. Tonight he was mixed up with one of the usual rush jobs and the deadline was for tomorrow afternoon. But if he went to sleep now he could get up early tomorrow and finish the assignment in time to satisfy the art director.

If he went to sleep now. That was downright comical. Sleep. As if sleep was something that came automatically. As if all he had to do was put his head against the pillows and close his eyes and go to sleep. He laughed without sound. He laughed at the picture of himself trying to sleep. Every night he had a debate with sleep and it was one rebuttal after another and it kept on like that until it knocked him out just about the time when the sun got started. That was his sleep.

He walked into the bathroom and saw himself in the mirror. Average height but on the husky side. Curly blond hair and quite a lot of it, so that was no worry. The worry came in where suggestions of silver showed here and there through the blondness. Very little silver, hardly noticeable against gold, but even the little that was there was too much silver for a man only thirty-three. And the lines under his eyes and around his lips, those lines weren't age. Those lines were ordeal. And even his complexion. It still retained considerable South Pacific, specifically Saipan and Okinawa, but the darkness of it was more shadow than sun. It seemed that there was shadow all over him, all around him.

More shadow moved in, and he decided to fight it. He took a shower and a shave, he put on a freshly cleaned and pressed palm beach suit. And he was getting his arm through a sleeve when he heard the noise from down the hall.

"A cop," a voice said. "Get a cop."

Another voice from out there. "What's the matter with you?"

"Get a cop."

Vanning's teeth came together, biting at nothing. He couldn't breathe. He stood there, waiting.

"What are you all excited about? What's wrong?"

"Who's excited? All I want is a drink. Bring me a cop of water."

"Why don't you learn to speak English?"

"Shut opp and bring me a drink of water."

From there on it became a typical husband-and-wife discussion, the wife yelling for a drink of water and continuing the yelling after she got it. Vanning used up a minute or so trying to decide whether they were Spanish or Italian or Viennese. He wondered when they had moved in. He wondered about all his neighbors. It was a point he made, keeping away from them. Keeping away from everybody.

He told himself to get a move on. He didn't know where he was going, but wherever it was, he was in a big hurry to get there.

Chapter Two

The heat came in waves, big rollers of heat wallowing in from all parts of Manhattan and down from a sky of melted asphalt. The heat flowed into Washington Square Park and stayed there despite a sporadic breeze. Vanning remained in the park only a few minutes. As he left the park, he aimed toward the corner of Christopher Street and Sheridan Square. There were a lot of lights in that direction, and he figured on a drink or two and maybe a chat with some unimportant person who would talk about unimportant things.

He was crossing a street and turning a corner when a man came up to him and asked for a light. There were no street lamps in this particular area and Vanning couldn't get a good look at the man. He could see, however, a small figure and a mustache and neatly combed black hair. He lit a match and applied it to the man's cigarette. And in the glow he obtained a fairly comprehensive view of the face. But it lasted only a moment. There was no special reason for analyzing the face.

"Hot night," the man said.

"Terrific."

"I saw some kids diving off the docks," the man said. "They got the right idea."

"If we did it," Vanning said, "people would call us crazy."

"The trouble with people is they don't understand people."

The man had a pleasant voice and a free-and-easy air, and Vanning told himself there was nothing unusual about the matter. The man merely wanted a light and a minute or so of chewing the rag, and if he was going to start worrying about all these little things he might as well put himself in a sanitarium.

The man leaned against a building wall. Vanning lit a cigarette for himself. They stood there like a couple of calm animals in a calm forest. The night was all around them and

4

the streets were quiet and the heat was dominant.

"I wonder how they stand it in the tropics," he said.

"They're born into it."

"I don't think I could stand it," the man said. "Ever been near the Equator?"

"A few times."

"What's it like?"

"Great," Vanning said. "You go nuts but you don't mind it, because everybody goes nuts."

"I've never traveled much."

"Don't go near the Equator," Vanning said. "This is twenty per cent of what it's like."

"When were you there?"

"During the war."

"I didn't get in," the man said. "A wife and kids."

"They put me in the Navy," Vanning said, and listened to himself saying it, and told himself to put a lock on his big mouth. He figured it was about time to start moving.

But the man said, "You see much action?"

"Enough."

"Where?"

"Around Borneo." He told himself it was all right. It would last maybe another minute and then he would tell the man he had to meet someone at Jimmy Kelly's or someplace and he would go away and the incident would fade into one of those vague little incidents that never make the front pages or the history books.

"I envy you," the man said.

"Why?"

"Farthest I've ever been away from New York is Maine. I used to go there summers, before things got tough."

"Hard going?"

"Lately," the man said.

"What's your line?"

"Research."

"Business?"

"More or less."

"I'm in advertising," Vanning said.

"Agency?"

"Free-lance artist."

"How do you fellows make out?"

"It runs in cycles. We don't know what we depend on. Maybe the sun spots."

"I think we're in for another depression," the man said.

"It's hard to say."

The man let his cigarette fall to the sidewalk. He stepped on it. "Well," he said, "I think I'll be going. She always waits up for me."

Vanning was about to let the whole thing pass, but he found himself saying, "Been married long?"

"Eleven years."

"I wish I was married."

"You say that as though you meant it."

"I do."

"It has its points," the man said. "In the beginning we were all set to break up. Times I'd be eating breakfast and there she'd be across the table and I'd wonder if it was possible to get rid of her. Then I'd ask myself why and I couldn't think of a good reason."

"Maybe the freedom angle."

"You're free."

"It gets monotonous. I think if you're normal you've got to have someone. You've got to have something special and it's got to be around all the time."

"Can't that get monotonous?"

"How do you feel about it?"

"Monotony's a relative thing."

"That isn't a pun, is it?"

"No," the man said. "I'm saying it in a positive way. You go out and look for a thrill and when you get it there's no thrill. The only thrill is looking for it. When you have someone you can look for a thrill together."

"Isn't that going a little deep?"

"I met her at a dance," the man said. "I had a devil of a time really getting to know her. She hadn't been around much, and you know how it is in New York. I bet you'll find more virgins in New York than any other town in the country. I mean in ratio. Even the little towns in the sticks. This is one burg where they build a defense mechanism at an early age. You can wear yourself out breaking it down. But don't get the wrong idea. That isn't why I married her."

"Why did you marry her?"

"I got to like her," the man said. "We had a lot of fun together. I don't know who you are and I'll never see you again in a hundred years, so it's all right to talk this way. I think it's a good idea to get things off your chest with strangers now and then."

"There's something to that."

"I developed a feeling for her," the man said. "I wanted to put my hands on her and at the same time I didn't want to do that and I got to thinking about it. It reached the point where I was buying things for her and I got a kick out of watching her face light up when she opened the packages. That had never happened before. We went around together for a little more than a year and then I went out and bought a ring."

"It always works that way."

"Not always," the man said. "I think I really fell in love with her about two years after the marriage. She was in the hospital then. We were having our first kid. I remember standing there at the bed, and there she was, and there was a baby, and I got all choked up. That was it, I guess. That was the real beginning."

"How many you got now?"

"Three."

"Three is just right."

"They're great kids," the man said. He raised a wrist toward his eyes and peered at the dial of a compact little watch. "Well," he said, "I've got to be running. Keep in trim."

"I will," Vanning said as the man started away. "Good luck."

"Thanks," the man said, and he was crossing the street. He turned a corner and walked up another block and crossed another street. A taxi came down the street in a listless way, the driver indifferent at the wheel, a cigarette miraculously hanging onto the driver's lips. The man raised his arm, waved it, and the taxi pulled toward the curb.

The man got in and gave the driver an address on the east side, slightly north of Forty-second Street, in the section known as Tudor City. The driver threw his cab into second gear and they were on their way.

In a little more than five minutes the man was home. He

had an apartment on the seventh floor of a place once in the high-rent category but now toned down a bit. In the elevator he lit a cigarette, glanced again at his wrist watch as he left the elevator, and saw the hands indcating a quarter to twelve. Walking down the hall, he took a key ring from his trousers pocket, and as he came to the door marked 714 he glanced once more at his wrist watch. Then he inserted the key, opened the door and entered the apartment.

It was a pleasant little place, definitely little for a family of five, but furnished to give an impression of more space. The main element was a large window that showed the East River. And there was a grand piano that had put him in the red for several months. There was a presentable secretary desk with some intelligent-looking books behind glass. The top row was given over to a set of The Book of Knowledge, but underneath that it was all strictly adult stuff. A good deal of Freud and Jung and Horney and Menninger, and some lesser-known works by other psychiatrists and neurologists.The kids were always standing on chairs to get at The Book of Knowledge, and once in a while they'd mess around with the other books and sometimes use crayon on the pages, but the top row was the only place for The Book of Knowledge because the other rows weren't high enough. There'd been a bit of discussion about that, especially when the six-year-old daughter had torn out all the pictures in one of the more involved and pathological works of Man's Nervous System, but there just wasn't enough room for another bookcase and it was rather useless to make a big issue over the matter.

He came into the living room and his wife put down a book and stood up and walked toward him.

"Hello, Mr. Fraser."

"Hello, Mrs. Fraser."

He kissed her on the cheek. She wanted to be kissed on the mouth. He kissed her on the mouth. She was an inch or so taller that he was, and she was on the skinny side and had the kind of face they use in fashion magazine ads where they don't want to concentrate too much on the face. It was an interesting face even though there was nothing sensational about it. It was interesting because it showed contentment but no smugness.

She put her hands on the sides of his head. She rubbed his temples. "Tired?"

"Just a little."

"How about a drink?"

"I could eat something."

"Sandwich?"

"No meat. Something light. God, but it's hot."

"I couldn't get the kids to sleep. They must be swimming in there."

"You look cool."

"I was in the bathtub an hour," she said. "Come on in the kitchen. I'll fix you something."

In the kitchen he sat down at a small white table and she began preparing a salad. It looked good to her and she added things to it and made enough for two. There was a pitcher of lemonade and she put more ice and sugar and water in it and sat down at the table with him.

She watched him as he tackled the salad. He looked up and smiled at her. She smiled back.

She poured some lemonade for him and as he lifted a forkful of lettuce and hard-boiled egg toward his mouth she said, "Didn't you have dinner?"

"Who can eat in this weather?"

"I thought we'd get a breeze from the river."

"Should have sent you and the kids to the country."

"We went through that."

"It isn't too late," he said.

"Forget about it," she said. "The hot spell's almost over."

"I could kick myself."

"We'll go next year."

"We said that last summer."

"Is it my fault?"

"No," he said, "it's mine. I'm sorry, honey, really I am."

"You know something?" she said quietly. "You're a very nice guy."

"I'm not nice at all. I was thinking of the money."

"They want too much these days," she said. "The prices they ask, they're out of their minds. Out on Long Island you should see what they're asking."

"I'm thinking of the country."

"You're worried about the kids."

9

"You and the kids."

"Oh, stop it," she said. "You're making enough."

"I'm making a fortune. Next week I'm buying a yacht."

She added some mayonnaise to her salad, mixed it in, ate for a while, and while concentrating on the food she said, "Anything new?"

"Still checking." He sipped some lemonade. "It's a tough one."

"Is he still there?"

"Still there. Tonight I talked to him."

"What happened?"

"I just talked to him. Nothing happened. He came out about eleven. Walked to the park. I followed him. He left the park and I walked up and asked for a match. That's about all."

"Didn't he say anything?"

"Nothing I could use. He's a difficult proposition. If there's anything criminal in that direction, I can't see it."

"Now, now—"

"I mean it, honey. He's got me buffaloed. For two cents I'd walk in and tell Headquarters they're on the wrong track."

"Suppose I gave you two cents?"

"I'd back out," he said.

She poured more lemonade into his glass. "I took your brown suit to the cleaner's. And you could use another pair of shoes."

"I'll wait till fall."

She studied his eyes. She said, "You never buy yourself anything."

"I do all right."

"You do fine," she said. She got up and walked toward him. Her fingers moved through his hair. "Someday you'll be important."

He smiled up at her. "I'll never be important," he said. "But I'll always be happy." He took her hand and kissed it and looked up at her again. "Won't we?"

"Of course."

"Sit on my lap."

"I'm gaining weight."

"You're a feather."

10

She sat on his lap. He drank some more lemonade and gave her some. She fed him a little more salad and took some herself. They looked at each other and laughed quietly.

"Like my hair?"

He nodded. He put his hand against her head, played with her hair. "You women have it tough in summer. All that hair."

"In winter it comes in handy."

"I wish it was winter already. I wish this case was over with."

"You'll get it over with."

"It's a problem."

She gave him a sideway smile. "And you eat it up."

"Not this one," he said. "This one's different. Something about this one gives me the blues. The way he talked. That tone. I don't know—"

She stood up. "I want to see if the kids are asleep."

Fraser lit a cigarette, leaned back a little to watch her as she crossed the living room. When the wall cut her off, he leaned forward and dragged deeply at the cigarette and stared at the empty glass in front of him. A frown moved onto his forehead and became more of a frown. The empty glass looked very empty.

Chapter Three

In this particular Village place there wasn't much doing. Four men at the far end of the bar were having a quiet discussion concerning horses. A young man and a young woman were taking their time with long, cool drinks and smiling at each other. A short, fat man was sullenly gazing into a glass of beer.

Vanning turned back to his gin rickey. A peculiar sense of loneliness came upon him, and he knew it was just that and nothing more. He wanted to talk to somebody. About anything. And again he saw himself in a mirror, this time the mirror behind the bar, and he saw in his own eyes the expression of a man without a friend. He felt just a bit sorry for himself. At thirty-three a man ought to have a wife and two or three children. A man ought to have a home. A man shouldn't be standing here alone in a place without meaning, without purpose. There ought to be some really good reason for waking up in the morning. There ought to be some impetus, there ought to he something.

Again one of those sighs got past his lips, and he recognized it and didn't like it. He was sighing that way too much these days. He finished the drink, downing the last few gulps too fast to get any real taste out of it, and then he ordered another drink and while waiting for it he saw the short, stocky beer drinker looking at him in a hesitant sort of way. It was evident that the fat fellow wanted to strike up a conversation, the fat fellow was lonely, too. Just then the drink arrived, another gin rickey.

Vanning offered the fat fellow a kindly smile, and the smile was appreciated and returned. Vanning moved his drink down along the bar, holding onto the smile, and said, "Well, this is one way of beating the heat."

The fat fellow nodded. "One thing I like about beer," he said. "It stays cold once it gets in you. Whiskey don't work that way."

"I guess whiskey's a winter drink," Vanning said, and suddenly he realized this was going to be an extremely dull conversation, and if he didn't push the topic onto another track they would be talking about liquor for the rest of the evening. He wondered what they ought to talk about and he considered baseball for a moment but had to discard it because he certainly wasn't up on his baseball. He didn't even know the league standings. It had been a long time since he had last opened a newspaper to the sports page.

And now, since there was nothing to say and nothing better to do, Vanning went to work on his drink.

The fat fellow said, "She's giving you the eye."

Vanning gulped and got it down. He looked at the fat fellow. He said, "What?"

"A number just walked in."

Vanning leaned far over the bar and studied the glass and its contents. Without fully knowing why, he said nastily, "Numbers are always walking in."

"This isn't bad."

"None of them are bad," Vanning said. "They're all wonderful."

"I just thought I'd mention it."

"Thanks," Vanning said. "Thanks for mentioning it."

The fat fellow shrugged and put some beer down his throat. He was quiet for a little while and then he said, "Too bad you're not interested."

"Why?"

"She is."

"That's nice," Vanning said. "It always builds the ego."

"I wish she was looking at me."

"Maybe I'm in the way."

"Oh, that's all right," the fat fellow said.

"No, really." And Vanning gave a brief, quiet laugh. "I'll move on down the bar. Or I'll take a walk outside. Anything you like."

"Don't do that. It wouldn't help me. I'm not her speed."

The nastiness cruised away. Vanning turned to the fat fellow and said sympathetically, "Now why carry on like that?"

"Oh, cut it out," the fat fellow said morosely. "I'm just a fat slob and I don't have enough brains to make people overlook it."

"Glands?"

"No, not glands. Appetite. I've had six meals already today and the night is still young. I'd have as much chance with that item as Eskimos in the Sahara."

"Go on," Vanning said, a little amused. "It isn't that hopeless. Give it a try. Nothing ventured—"

"Yes, I know all about that, and if I thought there was one chance in a thousand of getting a hello, I'd start an operation. But if I ever saw a hopeless state of affairs, this is it. I'm not in that league. Take a look at her and you'll see what I mean."

"Don't let them scare you," Vanning said, again lifting the glass. "They're not poison."

"Maybe you could sell me on that, but the way you say it, you don't mean it. You've been hurt, brother, you can't kid me. You've been hurt plenty."

Vanning's hand tightened around the glass. He put it down. He tapped ten fingers on the surface of the bar and

13

took a deep breath and gazed straight ahead. "All right," he said. "What about it?"

"Nothing," the beer drinker said. "I've been hurt too."

"That's a shame. Should we start crying on each other's shoulder or do you think maybe it's a good idea to skip the whole thing? Have another beer?"

"She sure is looking at you."

"All right, then," Vanning said, "don't have another beer. And do me a favor. Don't give me a play-by-play of what's taking place at the end of the bar."

"I bet I know what's the matter." And the fat fellow wore a gleeful, shrewd little smile. "You're one of those bashful guys. I bet you're afraid."

"Afraid?"

"That's what I said."

"Afraid," Vanning murmured. He gripped the rounded edge of the bar. "Afraid. I'm afraid."

The beer drinker waited a while, and then he said, "I beg your pardon, friend, but would you mind telling me what the hell is wrong with you?"

"I'm afraid," Vanning said.

"I'm going out for a sandwich," the fat fellow said. "Food settles all my problems, and yet my biggest problem is food itself. That's the way it goes, my friend, and I tell you it's a vicious circle, it certainly is."

"I guess so," Vanning said.

The fat fellow was paying his check, turning away from the bar, walking toward the door. Vanning watched him, and then Vanning's eyes hopped away and to the side and toward that part of the bar where she was standing alone in a yellow dress. Her figure was on the buxom side. Voluptuous, but in a quiet, wholesome way.

She was about twenty-six, Vanning estimated while he looked at her and while she looked directly back at him. And then the first coherent thought that entered his head was the idea that she didn't belong in this place, she ought to be home reading a good book, and tomorrow morning she ought to be in the park wheeling a baby carriage. And all that was in his eyes as he stood there looking at her, and agreement with all that was in her eyes as she looked at him.

Even at this distance he could see there was no paint on

14

her face except for some lipstick. But all the same there was color in her face, quite a bit of it aside from a beach tan, and it was deep rose all over her cheeks. He didn't think he was causing that. The deep rose was probably a permanent condition in her face. It was definitely a face, and it went along with the rest of her, and he knew why the fat fellow had retreated from the situation. The shining blond hair, loose and wispy and lovely around her shoulders, was something else that must have given the fat fellow a bad time.

She kept on looking at Vanning, and he kept on looking at her, and finally he told himself it was curiosity and nothing else that was making him pick up his drink, walk toward her.

Going toward her, it was more as though she were coming toward him, and the effect of her was something tremendous. He couldn't understand that, because along with it there was something uncanny, made all the more uncanny by the fact that she looked to be anything but uncanny or hard to figure out. He asked himself to stop trying to understand it.

He said, "Think you know me?"

"No."

"Then why are you looking at me?"

"Can't I look?"

He frowned and glanced at her with his head inclined a little. She stood there and looked at him. He had a feeling that she was a few strides ahead of him and he didn't like that.

"I guess you can look if you want to," he said. "I don't know what you expect to see."

"I'm not sure either."

"If you have a pencil and paper," Vanning said, "I'll be glad to write a short autobiography."

"That won't be necessary. But you can tell me what you do."

He laughed. It was a way to pass some time, anyway. That was what he told himself. He wasn't able to tell himself the truth. But the truth was there, inside him, and the truth was that a female in a few startling, swift moments, had gotten a hold on him and he had no inclination to free himself.

He said, "I paint."

"Houses?"

"Houses, horses, fountain pens, anything they want."

"Oh," she said, "then you're an artist."

"With apologies to Rembrandt."

"I didn't expect you'd be an artist. I thought—"

"Truck driver, longshoreman, heavyweight wrestler."

"Something along those lines."

"Disappointed?"

"Oh, no. Aren't artists glamorous?"

"I'm a commercial artist," Vanning said. "That means I'm a salesman, I'm part of a big selling job, and I actually get paid for painting pretty pictures."

"It sounds like a nice way to earn a living."

"It has its advantages," Vanning said. "But I do it all day long and at night I like to get away from it."

"I'm sorry."

"Don't be sorry. Talk to me. That's why I came in here."

"To see if you could meet a girl?"

"To see if I could find someone interesting to talk to."

"That's very strange," she said.

"How come?"

"I had the same idea."

"I don't think so," Vanning said. He got his eyes away from her and he watched his fingers rolling back and forth along the smooth roundness of the highball glass. "I think you came in here because you're an unhappy person, desperately unhappy and very disappointed with men, and probably disillusioned but not disillusioned to the extent that you're ready to throw all men aside. Do I hear the sound of a click?"

"Go on. Talk."

"Well"—Vanning went on playing with the glass—"I think you came in here a little on the frantic side, as if you're giving yourself a few last chances to meet someone worth while. Or maybe this was the final try. And you saw me standing there and you told yourself it was a bull's-eye if you could only attract my attention."

"Do all artists know this much about human nature?"

"I couldn't say. I don't hang around with other artists— Suppose we take one thing at a time. Suppose we talk about me after we get through with you. Is that all right?"

"If it isn't all right we'll do it anyway," she said. "Because you have your heart set on it. You're getting pleasure out of it."

"Not exactly what you'd call pleasure. But I think it would do us both some good if we skip the jockeying around. I mean come right out at the beginning and put it all on the table. That saves a lot of time. Sometimes it saves a lot of grief later on."

"What makes you think there will be a later on?"

"I didn't say there would be. What I'm really trying to do is catch up with you. I'm sure you're mature enough not to take offense at that."

She smiled. "My name is Martha."

"Jim."

"Hello, Jim."

"Hello. Have another drink?"

"I've had enough, thanks. Too much, I guess, on an empty stomach."

"We can fix that," Vanning said. "Come to think of it, all I had tonight was a sandwich and a malted."

He paid for the drinks and they walked out of the bar. Now it seemed that the heat was letting up a bit and the Hudson was sending over a breeze. Going toward midnight, the streets were quieting down and it was the bars and night clubs that were getting all the play.

Vanning looked at her. He said, "Got any special place in mind?"

"There's a little restaurant off Fourth Street. I don't know if it's still open."

"We'll try it."

The place was well off Fourth Street, and the weak yellow light from its window was the only light on the narrow street. Vanning took her in there and they sat at a small table near the window. They were alone in the place. It was very small. Their waiter was the proprietor, and he was a man who looked as if one of his own meals would do him a lot of good. He was trying to be friendly, but weariness prevented him from getting it across. He took their order and went away.

"All right," Vanning said, and he leaned toward her. "Now tell me."

17

"Yes, I've been married. Divorced. No children. I'm a buyer in a department store. Glassware. I live alone in a two-and-a-half here in the Village."

"I'll want that address. And the telephone number."

"Now?"

"Here's why. There's a slight possibility I might have to leave you in a hurry. Don't ask me to explain, but just on the chance that things work out that way, I'll want to see you again."

She opened a handbag, took out a pencil and a small pad. She did some writing and handed him the slip of paper. Without looking at it, he folded it and put it in his wallet.

"Now," she said, "what about you?"

"Never been married. I come from Detroit and I took engineering at Minnesota. If you like the rah-rah, I was an All-Western Conference guard. Then I was in Central America and we were showing them some new stunts with electricity and water power and so forth. While I was down there I began painting. For relaxation. Someone told me I could paint and I took him up on it. I did a lot of painting down there. Wind-up was engineering played second fiddle and I came back to the States and enrolled at an art school in Chicago. If there'd been a lot of money I would have gone in for the fine arts. But there was very little money and I had to go commercial. Things were breaking very nicely and the luck stayed with me all through those years and all through the war. I wasn't even scratched."

"Doing what?"

"Navy. I was a damage-control officer on a battleship."

A dull tone had crept into his voice and he wanted to get rid of it, he wanted to be amusing, diverting. He wanted to show her a nice time. He told himself this was a good thing, this thing happening to him now. She was something clean and refreshing; he felt sure this was the something he had sensed was going to happen tonight. He was glad, and yet there was a certain uneasy feeling along with that gladness, and he couldn't figure it out.

The food came and they ate silently. Every now and then he lifted his eyes and watched her for a moment or so. He liked the way she ate. A quiet sort of gusto. She took her time and yet she didn't waste any time. Her table etiquette was an easy, relaxed thing that made it a pleasure to sit here with her.

After the food, Vanning ordered peach cordials. They sipped the cordials and smiled at each other.

"I should be ashamed of myself," she said. "I mean, you picking me up like this. Or rather, me picking you up. But you called it right, Jim. I was very lonely, or let's even say desperate. I'll be looking forward to seeing you again."

"When?"

"Whenever you feel like seeing me."

"You don't know how good that sounds."

They finished their cordials and Vanning paid the check and they moved toward the door. They had to go down a few steps, because the door was below street level, with other steps leading up to the pavement, and now Vanning was opening the door, now they were going up the steps, now he knew something was wrong, he saw the shadow cutting in on light issuing from the restaurant, he saw the forms following the shadows and he told himself to twist away and race back into the restaurant and try a rear exit. But already it was too late for that, and the lateness was within him. He was angry, and the anger got the better of discretion, and he was going up the steps, taking her with him but not knowing she was there with him. And suddenly, as the three men came out of darkness and confronted him, he knew he had been expecting it. This was really it. This was the something he had expected would happen tonight.

The three of them stood up there at the top of the steps.

And one of them, his face half black, the other side of his face orange-yellow where the light hit it, smiled and took a cigarette from his lips, lowered his eyes toward Vanning and said, "Okay, bud. It's all over."

Her hand gripped his wrist, and he realized she was there, and along with that realization there was another, and it was a thunder burst; it made him blink, it made him stagger without budging. He took hold of her clutching hand, twisted her hand with violence, threw her away from him. She gasped.

There was a laugh from one of the men up there.

19

Vanning walked up the steps toward him. They stepped back to give him room, and yet they surrounded him, the three men and the girl beside him.

And then one of the men looked at Martha and said, "Thanks, honey, that was a beautiful piece of work."

"Yes," Vanning said. "It was terrific."

"You," said the man who had just spoken, and he smiled easily at Vanning, "you don't talk now. You do your talking later." Then he looked past Vanning, looked at the girl and said, "You can go home now, honey." He laughed with pure enjoyment. "We'll call you when we need you."

"All right," she said. "Do that."

Then she came walking up the steps and, coming abreast of Vanning, she looked at him with nothing in her eyes, and it lasted for an exploding second, and then she turned and walked away.

The three men closed in on Vanning. Two of them had their hands in the pockets of dark tropical worsted suits, but hands alone couldn't make the pockets bulge that much, and Vanning told himself to stop thinking in terms of a break.

One of the men said, "Let's take a little walk across the street."

The four of them crossed the street, walked down the block to where a large, bright green sedan was the only interference with thick midnight blackness.

The man who was doing most of the talking said, "Now we'll take a little ride." He climbed into the front seat. In the back, Vanning sat with a man on either side of him. His brain was empty. His mouth was dry and a coldness was getting itself settled within him, and now the car was in gear, going down the street, making a turn and picking up speed. They made a turn. They were going downtown, then they were swinging away from a wide street and going toward Brooklyn Bridge.

"If you tell us now," said the man behind the wheel, "we'll let you out and you can go home."

"I can picture that," Vanning said.

"Why don't you tell us now?" the man said. "You're going to tell us sooner or later."

"No," Vanning said. "I can't do that."

"You can't do that now, you mean. Because you're tough. But it won't last long. When we get to the point where you're not tough any more, you'll say what we want you to say."

"It isn't that," Vanning said. "I don't feel like getting myself hurt. If I knew, I'd tell you."

"Come off that," the man said. "That's in the heartache department. That's crying the blues. You know where you'll get with that? Nowhere."

"That's too bad," Vanning said. "Because then we'll both be nowhere."

"He's too tough," the driver said. "He's much too tough, I think. What do you say?"

"I say he's too tough," said the man who sat on Vanning's left. He was a big man and he wore glasses, and now he took them off very slowly, put them in a case and put the case in his pocket.

"What do you say, Sam?"

"Yes, he's too tough," said the man on the right, a short, wiry man with very little hair on his head. His arms were folded but slowly unfolding.

"I'm not tough at all," Vanning said. "I'm scared stiff."

"Now he's being funny," the driver said. They were on Brooklyn Bridge. The lights were whizzing in and passing the car, dropping other lights on sides of other cars, and all the light was bouncing around like captured lightning in a black vault.

"How about it?" Sam said.

"Hold it a second," the driver said. "Wait till we get off the bridge."

"I think the bridge is the best place," said the man who had been wearing glasses.

"We'll hold it awhile," the driver said. "Just for a little while, Pete, and then you can have your fun."

"Fun?" Vanning said.

"Sure," Pete said, and he laughed. "The bigger they are, the more fun they are."

"You mean with their hands and feet tied, don't you?"

"I can see you're going to be a lot of fun," Pete said.

The green sedan tore away from Brooklyn Bridge and went slashing into Brooklyn. It went through the city and

21

away from the city and into a section of vacant lots and shallow hills.

"I think now ought to be all right," Pete said. "What do you say, John?"

"Hold it awhile," the driver said.

"We're almost there," Sam said. "How about it, John? Just to get him accustomed to it."

"Maybe you're right," John said. "And then get him down on the floor and keep him there. I don't want him to see the layout until after we got him inside. So now, if you want to, you can go to work on him."

Pete twisted and threw a punch that hit Vanning on the side of the head, and an instant later Sam smashed him on the jaw, using brass knuckles. He lowered his head, testing the pain and the dizziness, feeling another blow and still another and yet another, and then he was going to the floor and they were kicking him. He wondered how long it would be until he lost consciousness. He looked up and saw the brass knuckles coming toward his face, and he threw himself to the side and the brass knuckles went past his head. Then the edge of a shoe caught him in the mouth and he realized there was only one way to stop this sort of thing. They weren't quite ready to kill him, and if be was going to get the slightest satisfaction out of this entire deal, now was the time to get it.

He came up from the floor, feinted at Pete, then swerved and let go with both hands, sending his fists into Sam's face. There was an opportunity for a follow-up, but instead of using it, Vanning swerved again, turned his attention to Pete. He leaned away from Pete's outstretched arm, then got under the arm, got his elbow under Pete's chin and heaved with the elbow, sending Pete's head quite a distance back, and then he hit Pete in the mouth, pistoned the same hand into Pete's mouth, then used both hands on Pete's face. That was about all he could do with Pete, because now Sam was showing a revolver and Sam was cursing and a lot of blood was flowing from Sam's nose.

"Bullets already?" Vanning said.

"Put the gun away," John said.

"I feel like blasting him." Sam was holding the gun a few inches away from Vanning's head.

"I told you to put the gun away," John said. "You're too fidgety with a gun, Sam. That's no good. I've told you that a lot of times. Give the gun to Pete."

"Sure," Pete said, the sound staggering through blood. "Let me have that gun."

"Be careful with it," John said. "We have a long night ahead of us. Just keep him covered and keep him on the floor."

Pete's foot thudded into Vanning's chest, forcing him against the floor and the front seat. "Stay there," Pete said. "Just stay there and regret the whole thing."

"I thought it was fun," Vanning said. "Didn't you?"

"The real fun hasn't started yet," Pete said.

The car made an acute turn, its wheels squealing. Vanning closed his eyes and told himself it was time to accept the thing for what it was. And it was very clear. It was very simple. Tonight he was going to lose his life. It was inevitable that someday this thing should catch up with him, and although he had sensed that all along, he had tried to stretch it as far as possible. That was a wholly natural way to take it and he couldn't condemn himself for acting in a natural way. All in all, it was one of those extremely unfortunate circumstances, and it had started on a day when it simply hadn't been his turn to draw good cards. He could have died on that day or on the day following or the week following. He could have died on any of those several hundred days in the months between then and now, so what it actually amounted to was the fact that all this time he had been living on a rain check and it was only a question of how long it would take until payday arrived.

The car was making turns, going long stretches without turns, making more turns, then sweeping around somewhere in a wide circle, slowing down.

"Put something around his eyes," John said.

"Why bother?" Sam said. "This is the last stop."

"Don't talk like that," Vanning said. "You make me feel blue."

"Bring your hand over here," Pete said. He was handing a large breastpocket handkerchief, folding it over, folding it again, then winding it around Vanning's head, drawing it tightly, knotting it.

23

"That's too tight," Vanning said.

"That's too bad," Pete said.

The car had stopped. They were getting out. They were taking Vanning across some sort of field. He could feel high grass brushing up against his ankles. Then the high grass gave way to hard-packed soil and it went on that way for a few minutes, and then they were walking up steps that had to be wood because there was considerable creaking. After that the sound of a key in a lock, the sound of a door opening, the feeling of entering a large room, going through the room with big hands pushing him, holding him back, pushing him again. Now a stairway, a long climb, and now a corridor, and then another door opening, and the sound of a wall switch and light getting through the fabric that covered his eyes. He was working his lips toward a smile. He managed to build the smile. There was some fatalism in it, and a trace of defiance. And underneath the smile he was terribly frightened.

Chapter Four

Lavender light came down on a purplish river. There was a huge ferry boat crammed with people. The ferry had shut off its power and was floating toward the wharf when suddenly a monster wave came from noplace and hit the ferry on starboard and knocked it over on its back. And there were no people to be seen. Only the ferry, floating on its back. And the river, calm again. And Fraser twisted his face against the pillow and let out a groan. He opened his eyes. He closed them again, opened them again and saw his wife sitting up beside him, looking at him.

"You're all worked up," she said.

"What was I doing?"

"Making noise."

"Did I say anything?"

"I couldn't make it out. Can I get you something?"

"No," Fraser said. "Just put on the light."

She switched on a lamp at the bedside. Fraser blinked and rubbed his eyes. He reached toward a table near his side of the bed, fumbled with a pack of cigarettes and a book of matches. She didn't want a cigarette. She wanted him to go back to sleep. Lighting his cigarette, he got out of bed, walked to the window and looked out. The East River was glimmering black pitch and the lights were points of spears lancing a smoldering night.

He took several short puffs at the cigarette. "I can't get it out of my mind."

"You should be on time and a half for overtime," she said. "You work twenty-four hours a day."

"Not always."

"Want a drink of water?"

"I can get it."

"Let me get it."

She climbed out of bed, and Fraser was alone in the room and he wanted to get dressed and leave the apartment. He was putting on his socks when she came back with the water. She let him finish the water and then she picked up his shoes and took them back to the closet.

"Take off your socks," she said, "and stop the nonsense."

"I feel like doing something."

"On what basis?"

"I don't know," Fraser said.

"I wish you'd get yourself a job in Wall Street. Keep this up and you'll be gray in no time."

She sat down beside him on the edge of the bed. She put a hand on his shoulder. For a while they sat there quietly, then Fraser got up and walked to his dresser. He opened the top drawer of the dresser and took out a brown paper portfolio and began extracting paraphernalia. He stood there at the dresser, studying various papers.

This went on for several minutes, and then she came toward him. He looked at her, and she had her arms folded and she was saying, "Now stop it."

"Go back to sleep."

"I can't sleep with the light on."

"Put on your eyeshade."

"You're being inconsiderate."

"I'm sorry," Fraser said. "I can't help this."

"What is it?" she said. "What's all the fuss?"

"So many angles I can't figure."

"Tomorrow. Please, dear. Tomorrow."

"You go back to sleep. I'll go in the other room."

She went back to the bed. Fraser walked out of the room. In the living room he switched on the light and sat down with the paraphernalia. A few minutes later she came into the living room.

"I can't sleep," she said, "when you are't sleeping."

He picked up the papers and began putting them back in the portfolio. "All right," he said, "I'm done now."

She stopped him. "No, you're not. You won't close your eyes all night. Sit here. Talk to me. Tell me."

Fraser smiled at her. "You've got a very nice nose."

"It's too thin."

"I think it's very nice." He ran his finger along the bridge of her nose. Then he looked away from her and began punching a fist into a palm, punching lightly, steadily. "They're letting me do it my own way," he said. "If I ruin it, it's my own fault, mine alone. I'm sure I know where I'm going, but I'm not infallible. No man is."

"Don't make excuses to me. I'm a college graduate. I understand things."

Fraser let out a sigh. "It's a very difficult setup. It's like one of those cryptograms where the more steps you solve, the harder the rest becomes."

"You'll work it out."

"I wonder."

"You mean that, really?"

He looked at her. He nodded slowly. "It's a bad one, honey. It's definitely a bad one. With what I've got now, I can turn him in tomorrow. With what they have on him already, they can put him on trial and it's a hundred to one he'd get a death sentence. That's why I find it a little hard to sleep."

"Put if that's what he deserves—"

"If."

"Is that your worry?"

"Not under ordinary conditions. But this is a very unusual state of affairs. The record says the man's a bank robber. A murderer. It adds and it checks and it figures. They've got witnesses, they've got fingerprints, they've got a ton of logical deduction that puts him in dead center. And what I've got is a mental block."

"What is this, the old humane element?"

"Just a theory."

"You've got a theory and they've got the facts."

"I know," Fraser said. "I know, I know." He rubbed the back of his head. "If I could only talk to him. I mean really talk. If I wasn't in such a delicate spot. It's one hell of a jam, and every time I walk into Headquarters they look at me with pity."

"You need help on this one."

"I need a miracle on this one."

"You're doing all you can."

"That's what bothers me," Fraser said. "The best shadow job I've ever done. Know every move he makes. Got it down to a point where I can leave him at night and pick him up when he walks out in the morning. I know what he eats for lunch, what kind of shaving cream he uses, how much money he makes with the art work. I know everything, everything except what I need to know."

"He's just clever."

"He's not clever," Fraser said. "That's another thing. I'll be dogmatic about that. He's intelligent, but he's not clever. Talk about a paradox, this one takes the cake."

"You're not a mind reader. You're not an adding machine. You've only got one brain and one set of eyes. Stop trying to knock yourself out."

Fraser stood up. He walked across the living room and came back to the sofa and looked at the wall. "It's a shame," he said. "It's a damn shame."

"What is?"

"They had to go and lose track of those others. That's what they get for putting two-bit operators on a big case. When I think of how they fumbled—"

"That's their fault, not yours."

"It's my fault if Vanning gets the chair."

"What makes you so sure he's innocent?"

"I'm not sure."

"Then what are you worried about?"

"For a college graduate that's a foolish question."

"Are you quarreling with me?"

"I'm quarreling with myself."

She pulled him down to the sofa. She put her hands against the sides of his head and made him look at her. "Let me fix you some tea."

"Black coffee."

"I said tea."

"All right, tea."

She walked into the kitchen. Fraser sat there on the sofa for a while and then went into the kitchen. She was standing at the stove.

He stood behind her and said, "Can I bore you awhile?"

"Please do."

He took a very deep breath. "Here's one for Aesop," he said. "Three men rob a bank in Seattle. They run away with three hundred thousand dollars. They get as far as Denver. In Denver they register at a hotel under assumed names. They have a contact man in Denver, a smooth manipulator named Harrison. This man Harrison has the job of taking the money, getting it in a safe place or putting it in various channels or something. You follow me?"

"I've heard this a thousand times."

"Hear it again. The Harrison party comes to the hotel. He walks out with one of the men, a personality registered under the name of Dilks. Now get this, because this part was witnessed. Dilks was carrying a small black satchel. The money. All right, all that's under the heading of fact. Now we go into theory."

"Yours?"

"No, Headquarters'. Harrison and Dilks take a little stroll. And somewhere long the line this Dilks gets a bright idea. He decides three hundred thousand is a neat little sum and why give it to Harrison? Why not keep it for himself? He waits until he and Harrison are on a dark, quiet street and then he pulls a gun and kills Harrison. He runs away and hides the money. Now we leave theory and come back to fact."

"Here's your tea."

"Put it on the table. Listen. Dilks gets out of Denver. But he leaves fingerprints on the gun found near Harrison's body. He leaves a blue convertible with a California license. Police go to work and start checking. And they find out this man Dilks is not Dilks at all, he's a former Navy officer named James Vanning. They start looking for him."

"Lemon?"

"Just a drop. On a night like this I need hot tea."

"It's good for you. They say it's the best thing in hot weather."

"Do you want me to go on?" Fraser said. And she nodded soberly and he said, "They rack their brains trying to figure this Vanning. No former record, nothing except a few minor traffic violations, and that from way back. Before the war he was a commercial artist in Chicago. Made a fairly nice living at it. Why does this man rob a bank? Why does he commit a murder?"

"A lot of men came back from the war and had the wrong outlook and got themselves in trouble."

Fraser nodded. "That's what Seattle says. That's what Denver says. That's what Headquarters says. Maybe they're right."

"And so?"

"Maybe they're wrong. Now look, do you want to hear the rest of this?"

"I'm not interrupting." She gave him an indignant look. "I'm just discussing it with you."

Fraser stirred the sugar in his teacup. He blew on the tea and took an experimental sip. "Too hot," he said. "I'll let it cool for a while." He took another deep breath and leaned forward. "They look for Vanning. They can't find him. They look for the other two men. No trace. A time interval, and then we see these two other men here in Manhattan. We follow them. We're about to pick them up and then we get very brilliant and we lose them.

"And then we get a call from someone who spots a man answering Vanning's description. We check. It's Vanning. And Headquarters wants to move in, but Seattle does't feel like losing three hundred thousand and there's the factor of making sure. Headquarters disagrees with Seattle, but Seattle claims it would be a very nice thing if the money was picked up along with Vanning. Of course Denver puts up a kick because Denver wants to wrap up a murder case. There's something of a delay and then they give me the assignment and I'm supposed to settle this little discussion between three cities.

"So I focus on Vanning. I wait. I wait some more. I follow him like I've never followed anyone. And I wait. I wait for some indication of a lot of money being spent or hidden or invested. No indication. Nothing. Just Vanning from day to day, and if I don't hurry up and come in with something they'll give me orders to grab him."

"And they'll be right."

"No, they won't be right. They'll be making a terrible mistake. Why did those other men come to New York? Because Vanning's here. They trailed him. They know he's somewhere in town and they're looking for him. They want that money. If we take Vanning, we lose the chance of an established contact between him and those other men. Headquarters says forget about those other men, but I've got the feeling we'll never wind up this case if we don't grab all three."

"But isn't Vanning the killer?"

"Yes."

"That's definite?"

"Yes."

"In your own mind?"

"Yes."

"Well, then?"

Fraser lowered his head. He hit his fists against the table. "I don't know, I can't get rid of the notion. He's a killer and yet he's not a killer."

She leaned her head sideways and gave her husband a careful look. "Is this man your cousin or something?"

He picked up the teacup and took a few gulps. "I wish you'd try to follow me. If I thought this was a hunch or a brain storm I'd laugh at myself. But it's so much deeper than that." He leaned across the table. "I know Vanning. For months now I've been walking behind him, watching every move he makes. I've been in his room when he wasn't there, when I knew it would take him a half-hour to finish a restaurant meal. I've been with Vanning hour after hour, day after day. I've been living his life. Can't you see? I know him, I know him. I"—and the rest of it came out in a low tone, rapid and strained—"I understand him."

She got up from the table and gathered the teacups and took them toward the sink. She turned the faucet handle and the water came out in too much of a rush. She turned it down a little. Quickly, efficiently, the cups were washed and dried and she put them back in the kitchen cabinet. As she closed the door of the cabinet she heard him getting up from the table and she turned to see him walking out of the kitchen. She started to follow him, but just then her eye caught the top of the smooth white table and there was something on the table that caused her to frown. She moved toward the table.

She had seen this sign of extreme agitation once before on a night when their youngest child, stricken with pneumonia, had been approaching the crisis.

She stood there at the table and looked at the scraps of fingernail.

Chapter Five

"All right," John said. "Let him see where he is."

The blindfold was removed. Vanning blinked a few times and then he looked at John. It was the same John. The same hunched shoulders, rather wide, the same creased leathery face and large, flat nose and thick lips that didn't have very much blood in them. The same stringy necktie. Everything the same, even the way John wore his hair, a salt-and-pepper brush that covered his head like a mat of steel wool.

John put a cigarette in his mouth and lit it. He seated himself on the edge of a studio couch. Sam and Pete were up against the wall, standing there like statues. That left Vanning in the center of the room, with light from the ceiling doing a slow fall onto the top of his head. There was some pain in his face from the brass knuckles, and there was a quantity of dizziness, but not so much that he couldn't stand there balancing himself on two feet. He turned his back on the two men who stood against the wall. He looked at John.

"Well?" John said.

"Your move," Vanning said.

They were gazing at each other as if they were alone in the room. John leaned back on an elbow, crossed one leg over the other and took a long, contemplative haul at the cigarette. He blew out the smoke in a single quick exhalation and said, "All I want is the cash."

"I don't know where it is."

"Now say that again," John said. "Just say it to yourself and hear how foolish it sounds."

"I know it sounds foolish, but that's the way it is and I can't help it."

John looked at the black-and-white shoes, the suit and shirt and blue-and-black tie and he said, "Nice clothes you have on."

"I like them."

"They cost money."

"They're not bad clothes," Vanning admitted. "But they're not the real high quality. Not the kind of quality I'd be wearing if I had that cash you're talking about."

"It's a point," John said. "But not much of a point. What are you doing these days?"

Vanning liked that question. It was more of an answer than a question. It told him something he was hungry to know, and it offered a foundation for some strategy.

He said, "Nothing much." He tossed a few ideas around in his head, selected one of them and added, "I have a photo studio uptown, West Side, I manage to make a living, and there's a studio couch and a bathroom, and that way I save on rent."

John looked at the floor and blew some smoke toward a faded violet rug. Vanning studied John's face and told himself it had been a clever play. At least he understood now they didn't know where he was living. He put it together rapidly. They had spotted him in the Village. Followed him. Made a fast contact with the girl and told her to work on him, to get him out of the bar and out of that street and into the restaurant on the dark and empty street. It was reasonable. It checked. It was a typical John manipulation. Because John had just so much brains and no more. John wasn't exactly a fool, but he was harder than he was clever, and probably he knew that about himself, because he had a habit of laboring to be clever.

"Look," John said. "You've got a fair amount of intelligence. You're on one side and I'm on the other. That's clear

32

enough. So we'll take it from there. It's got to be managed along those lines. In order for you to stay alive and have a happy life ahead of you, what you have to do is tell me where you put that cash, then we keep you here until I have the cash, and then we let you go. Does that make sense?"

"It would make wonderful sense," Vanning said, "except that I don't know where that cash is located and that's why I can't tell you. Now does that make sense?"

"No, it doesn't. I can see a man misplacing a ten-dollar bill. Maybe even a hundred-dollar bill. But it doesn't figure that a man will let three hundred thousand dollars slip out of his fingers just like that. And that brings us to another angle. If you really lost the money, you lost it in Colorado. And that means you wouldn't be here if you didn't have the money. You'd still be in Colorado, looking for it."

"Colorado is a big place."

"Three hundred thousand dollars is a lot of money. Most people I know would use a magnifying glass and search every inch of the state."

"Maybe you and I don't know the same kind of people."

John threw the cigarette onto the floor, waited until it burned the rug, then stepped on it. He looked at the mashed stub. He said, "We're not getting anywhere." Then he looked up at Vanning without raising his head. "Are we?"

Vanning sighed. "We can't get any further than this. I don't know where it is. I tell you I don't know where it is."

"Don't get excited," John said. "We have plenty of time."

"I don't look at it that way. If I did, I'd try to stall. I'd try to bargain. I'd ask for some assurance that you'd leave me alone after you had the money, and I'd give you assurance that I'd leave you alone."

"You wouldn't have to do that," John said. "We know you'd leave us alone. We know you wouldn't go to the law. How could you go to the law when the law is looking for you?"

Vanning frowned. "What do you mean, looking for me?"

"You're wanted for murder," John said. "Didn't you know that?"

"You're way ahead of me," Vanning said. "I don't remember murdering anybody."

John smiled with understanding and patience and

allowed it to coast for a while. Then he beckoned with his fingers and said, "Come on, come on."

Vanning, without moving his head, could see part of the window at his side, and he wondered if he could make it in leap He wondered how far it was to the ground. With a big effort he got his mind away from the window and he said, "How much do you know?"

"We know you killed him," John said. "We know the law has you tagged. People saw you with him that night. So the law found out what you looked like. And the car license. That was another thing. Your description tallied with the description of the car owner. And still another thing, the big thing. You bought the car in Los Angeles and you got a license there. That gave them a record of your fingerprints, and the prints checked with prints on the gun."

"How do you know all this?"

"It's the kind of news that gets around," John said. "Newspapers and people talking and so forth. We hung around in Denver for a while, and then we picked up on you from a tip that came from New Orleans. Later we got another tip from Memphis. And then a third tip from New York. We figured you'd stay in New York for quite a time. It's a nice place to hide. What happened was you were spotted in a Village bar. The man who made the contact had to go and lose you in a traffic jam, but we figured we'd tag you again, sooner or later. And that's the way it adds, so now maybe we can come to terms."

"I wish we could," Vanning said. "I wish I had something to offer."

"Put yourself in my place," John said. "I'm very hungry for that cash. I'm so hungry that I'm willing to give you a slice. Say fifty thousand. How does it sound?"

"It sounds great. That's what makes this picture so miserable. I just don't know where that money is."

John stood up. He said, "Final?"

"Final," Vanning said.

"No," John said. "I don't think so." He looked at the two men who stood motionless against the wall.

"Well?" Pete said.

"All right." John was walking toward the door. "You can have him now."

Beyond the pain, beyond the spinning and all the gleaming red, and beyond the falling rocks that crushed and clanged and beyond the black flood shot with more red, with some livid purple in there beyond all that, there was a stillness and it was the stillness of memory, and he groped his way toward it. And he came out in the bright gold of a springtime afternoon in Colorado, and on the pale blue convertible coupe he had bought in Los Angeles after receiving his discharge, he was driving toward Denver with the idea that he would stay in Denver for a while and then take his time going up to Chicago.

The convertible purred its way along the mountain road, and the radio purred along with it, Noro Morales handing out a suave rhumba. The top was down and the sky was very clear and it was good to know that the war was over and that agency in Chicago was the kind that kept its promises, a big firm with stability and energy, and they had liked his work and in reply to his letter they had told him to come on back and go to work. They asked him if seventy-five hundred a year was all right. He was thinking, before the war they had paid him five thousand a year. That was the kind of outfit it was. He felt good about going back. He felt good about everything. Chicago was an all-right place, and someday in the not too far distant future he ought to be meeting a nice girl and getting married and starting a home. It was a fine thing to be thirty-two and alive and healthy. It was a marvelous thing to be starting fresh.

He whistled along with Noro Morales and the convertible floated along the road.

Suddenly, away up there ahead of him, where the road went curving its way up along the mountain, there was a violent noise, and it sounded as if an automobile had crashed into something. Vanning pressed hard on the accelerator and the convertible leaped, and it took a few turns, made a whizzing straightaway run as the road sliced into a tunnel, came out to make another turn, then he saw a branching road, very narrow, almost at right angles to this road, and saw a wreckage.

It was a station wagon and it was turned over on its side against a rock. Two men were stretched out on a patch of bright green near the rock, and a third man in his shirt sleeves was leaning against the rock.

Vanning turned the convertible onto the narrow road and raced it toward the scene of the accident. As he brought the convertible to a stop, the man who was still upright came walking toward him. The man had a leathery face and hair that looked like a mat of steel wool. There was a leather contrivance under the man's left shoulder and it was held there by straps, and now the man reached toward it, took something out of it, came up to Vanning and pointed the revolver in Vanning's face.

"Get out of the car," the man said. "Give me a hand."

"Why the gun?"

"I said get out of the car."

Vanning climbed out of the convertible and the man walked along with him. The two men on the ground were moving about and groaning. One of them, a big man with glasses hanging from one of his ears, was slowly forcing himself to a sitting position, adjusting the glasses and staring around stupidly. The other man, small and wiry and getting bald, was out cold.

The man with the gun was saying, "How is it, Pete?"

"I think I'm all right," the big man said. "Had the wind knocked out of me." He looked at Vanning. "Where did you pick this up?"

"He just came along."

The big man inclined his head to get a look at Vanning's automobile.

"It's a lucky break," the big man said.

"Yeah, we're overloaded with luck today," said the man with the gun. He looked at the smashed station wagon. "Overloaded. Take the gun and keep it on this guy. I'll have a look at Sam."

"Maybe we ought to hurry," Pete said.

"That's why we smashed up. We were in too much of a hurry. Press the gun on him. He looks nervous."

"Why should I be nervous?" Vanning said.

"You shut up," Pete said. He prodded the gun against Vanning's spine, held it there. A few moments later he said, "How does it look, John?"

"I think he's done for," said the man with steel-wool hair.

"I think he busted his head. But he's still breathing."

"You think he'll last long?"

"I can't say."

"I always told you Sam was a lousy driver. I told you he was no good in a squeeze."

"Close your head. I'm trying to think what we should do."

"Should we leave him here?"

"That's why I asked you to close your head. Because every time you open your mouth you prove you were born without brains. How can we leave him here? Look at him. He's still alive."

"I know that, John, but you just claimed he won't last long. What's the use of letting him suffer? We'll be doing him a favor if we put a bullet in him. All I got to do is—"

"Keep that gun where it is," John said. "And keep your head closed while I figure this out."

Just then the man on the ground let out a loud groan and opened his eyes.

"I don't know, John. We ain't got much time," Pete said.

John looked down at the man on the ground. He said, "Sam, you drive like a monkey."

Sam let out another groan and closed his eyes.

"You," John said, and he pointed at Vanning, "you come over here and lend a hand."

"Wait a minute," Pete said. "What do you figure on doing?"

"What does it look like?"

"We can't take Sam with us," Pete said. "He'll slow us down."

"Sure, that's right," John said. "And if we leave him here and they find him and he's still alive, the first thing he'll think of is that we left him. I don't think he'll appreciate that. You never know. He might even open his mouth."

"But if he's dead he won't be able to open his mouth."

"What's the matter, Pete? Don't you like Sam?"

"I get along with Sam. You know that. But why take chances?"

"We won't shoot him," John said. "And we won't talk about it any more. We're taking him with us and if we can find a doctor somewhere we'll see if he has a chance." He

37

glanced up at Vanning. "All right, you. Let's go to work."

Vanning and John carried the injured man to the convertible, placed him in the back seat. Then John ran back to the wrecked station wagon, got inside and came out, carrying a black satchel. He brought it back to the convertible, threw it on the floor near the front seat and said to Vanning, "Get in there and put the top down."

"What do you want with me?" Vanning said. "Why don't you take the car? Leave me here."

"And have you describe the car to the law?" John smiled in appreciation of his own strategy. He shook his head. "Nothing doing. You come with us. And you drive. Pete, you stay in the back seat and look after Sam."

"I still think," Pete said, "it would be better if I put a bullet in Sam."

"I think," John said, "you ought to cut out that line of thought."

"It ain't that I have anything against him. It's just that I—"

"Come on," John said. "Let's be on our way."

They were in the car now, the top was down, the car was rolling. It made a turn onto the other road, it ran down the other road, and the road ran up and out and once more skirted the side of the mountain. Vanning watched the rearview mirror.

"You keep your eyes on the road," John said.

"I'm getting a little nervous," Vanning said.

"So am I," John said, and he brought up the revolver so that Vanning could see it was still around. "Suppose we both calm down and then maybe nothing will happen."

"Should I put on the radio?"

"No," John said. "I'll entertain you. I'll tell you a little story. Once upon a time there were three bad men. They were very bad. They robbed banks. In Seattle they robbed a bank and got away with three hundred thousand dollars in thousand-dollar notes. Then they stole a station wagon and scooted out of Salt Lake City. Then they were chased and they had to go fast. They went so fast that their station wagon smashed up. But a kind man came along and helped them out. He had a blue automobile and he was very good-natured about the whole thing."

From the back seat Pete's voice came whining in, "I don't see why you have to tell him about the three hundred grand."

"I'll tell him what I feel like telling him," John said. "I got the funny feeling he's going to be with us for a while." He turned to Vanning. "How about it? Would you like that?"

"I'd love it," Vanning said.

"Turn off at the next crossing," John said. "There's a road brings us into Leadville. There's a doctor in Leadville—anyway, I think it was Leadville—it was a long time ago, but this doctor, if I remember correctly, he was willing to talk business. Anyway, we'll try Leadville."

A quarter of an hour later the blue convertible arrived in Leadville and cruised around for a while, and John was trying to remember where the doctor was located.

Finally they pulled up in front of a hotel and John went in and came out a few minutes later and they went on down the street, made a turn, stopped in front of a wooden structure that had given up the fight a long time ago. John got out of the car, looked up and down, waited for two middle-aged women to cross the street and go on to another street, and then he gestured to Pete. While Pete carried Sam out of the car, John entered the dead house, his gun nudging Vanning, who walked along just a bit ahead of him as they came into the hallway.

The doctor wanted five hundred dollars now and another five hundred to be paid in three weeks, at which point Sam would be ready to travel again. John paid the doctor and then he and Vanning and Pete left the house and got back into the car.

"Now we'll go to Denver," John said.

They arrived in Denver just as the sun was starting to drop. They went into a small hotel in a shabby part of town and they were given a fairly large room on the third floor. John sent a boy out for liquor. The boy came back with liquor and ice and bottles of ginger ale and several packs of cigarettes. John gave the boy a dollar bill and Vanning looked at the boy, but the boy was looking at the dollar bill and then the boy was walking out of the room, the door was closing, the door was closed, the room was quiet.

John opened a bottle and went to work with ice and

ginger ale. Pete was stretched out on the bed, and every few moments Pete would complain about Sam and whine that he didn't like the Sam angle. Finally John told Pete that if he didn't keep quiet he would be hit over the head with a liquor bottle.

"I can't help worrying," Pete said.

"Go out and get some air," John said. "Do your worrying outside. No. Wait a minute. I have another idea. Stay here. Hold the gun on him a minute. I want to look in the bathroom."

"What's in the bathroom?" Pete said.

"Usually a skylight, when it's on the top floor."

Pete looked at Vanning, pointing the gun at Vanning. "We ain't on the top floor."

"I'll make sure," John said. "Hold the gun on him."

John went into the bathroom, came out and said, "It's all right. No skylight, no windows." He smiled at Vanning. "Get in there."

Vanning walked into the bathroom. They closed the door on him. He could hear them talking in the next room. All at once their voices dropped, and although he had his ear pressed against the door crack, he couldn't make it out. The low-toned conversation went on for quite a while. And then it faded and there was nothing and the nothing went on for a very long time and Vanning couldn't understand that.

He stood at the door and said, "How long do you figure on keeping me here?"

There was no answer.

He said, "It's getting stuffy in here."

No answer.

"At least," he said, "you might let me have a cigarette."

Nothing.

"Anyway," he said, "a drink."

And there was no answer.

And he said aloud, "Maybe you're not even there. Maybe you went out for a walk."

No answer.

"All right," he said. "I'll find out."

He opened the door and stood there looking at the empty room.

The room was terribly empty. The door was closed. And the room was empty. It was good. And that was why it was bad. It was too good. What made it ridiculously good was the revolver that calmly gazed back at him as he stared at it where it rested, emphatically black against the white bed-spread. He walked to the bed, picked up the revolver and put it in his coat pocket. For no good reason at all he walked to the window and looked out. He saw an alley, a dark sky and nothing else. He moved across the room and picked up a half-empty bottle of whiskey and looked at it and put it down. He picked up a ravaged pack of cigarettes and put one of them in his mouth. He didn't quite know what to do. He told himself that a little calm reasoning ought to get him at the source of this. And he sat on the bed, looked at the floor and tried to reason calmly.

What they should have done, if they were smart, was to get him alone somewhere, out in the woods or on a dark street, and then kill him in a hurry and take themselves out of Denver. That was the way to do it without complication. This business of walking out on him, leaving him here alone, leaving the revolver on the bed, it added up to an odd maneuver, and the only way to find the answer was to put himself in their place and think along the same lines as they would think. He told himself he ought to be intelligent enough to box with them, as long as they were in the mood for boxing. He told himself, despite the fact that he and John were in two widely separated fields of endeavor, he ought to be able to outwit John, anyway draw up even with John.

Knowing that liquor wouldn't help, he decided to have a drink, regardless. He stood up, walked toward the dresser where the bottles and ice were assembled, and then he stopped dead, at first frowning, then widening his eyes until they hurt, and then frowning again. And he was staring at the top of the dresser, not staring at the bottles, but staring at the satchel.

There it was, right there in front of him. The black satchel that John had taken out of the station wagon. A new satchel of finely grained leather. Whatever was in it was filling it, making it strain with bulging. He knew what was in it. He told himself he didn't know what was in it. He told himself

41

to leave the satchel alone, put the gun back on the bed, get out of here and get out of Denver. And do it fast and get it started now. Hurry on to Chicago, go to work at the drawing board, meet a nice girl and start a home. Leave the satchel alone. Leave it alone.

"Use your head," he said aloud. "Leave it alone."

He rubbed his hands into his eyes. His teeth clicked and clacked. His head was lowered and then he was shaking his head.

"Come on," he said. "Come out of it."

And then he raised his head and locked at the satchel. It was there, fat and black and shiny and bulging. There was something luscious about it. It looked very strong, sitting there on top of the dresser.

Vanning moved toward the dresser, his hands stretching toward the satchel, then suddenly veering away, clutching at the nearest bottle. He worked whiskey into a highball glass, studying the amount of whiskey he had poured, telling himself he had never taken that much whiskey in a single drink. He took the glass toward the bathroom door, leaned against the door, looked at the satchel, kept his eyes on it as his head went back, as he raised the glass toward his mouth. Then his eyes were closed and the whiskey was flowing down his throat, exploding in his belly. And the empty glass fell out of his limp hand and hit the floor and made considerable noise as it cracked apart.

The noise echoed within Vanning's brain. He told himself to go to the window and lean out and call for help. Then he laughed at himself. He laughed out loud. The sound of it was attractive in an eerie way and he laughed harder. Maybe if he laughed loud enough, someone would come in and see him here and talk to him. He wanted that badly right now. If he only had someone in here with him, someone with whom he could discuss this. He stared at the satchel.

He rubbed his hands together, telling himself he looked like a safety man waiting for a punt. Then he walked toward the dresser. He rubbed his hands again. He took hold of the satchel, lifted it, brought it over to the bed and opened it and saw United States currency.

Thousand-dollar bills. In small packets, ten bills in each

packet, and he counted thirty packets. That made three hundred thousand dollars, he told himself. He placed the packets in the satchel, closed it and stared at it.

Then he came bounding up from the bed, and he picked up the satchel and walked out of the room. He walked down the hall toward the stairway. Just before he reached the stairway someone moved in behind him, something pressed against his side. And the party said, "Keep walking. Be good."

Vanning turned his head and he was looking at a man he had never seen before. The man wore a white panama and a pale green suit, a dark green shirt and yellow tie and a yellow handkerchief flowing largely, gracefully, from the breast pocket. The man was tall and heavy, and he had a square face and his skin was sun-darkened.

"Just keep walking," the man said. "Downstairs and to the right and we'll go out through a side door."

"You can have the money," Vanning said.

"I don't want the money."

"Are you a policeman?"

The man let out a laugh that suddenly got itself sliced clean. "Just keep walking," he said.

They arrived on the second-floor landing. The gun nudged Vanning's side, then pressed hard, and Vanning winced, and then he was going downstairs with the man that way beside him, the gun that way against him, and they were in the lobby and a few people were standing around doing nothing the way only people in hotel lobbies can do nothing.

"So help me," the man said, "if you let out a whimper I'll let you have it. Now go toward that side door as if you're going out with me for a stroll."

They went toward the side door, the man opened the door, they walked out and down a dark street, and nothing was said until the man told Vanning to make a turn. A minute later he told Vanning to make another turn. They were on a narrow street, weakly illuminated by yellow light coming from second-story windows.

"Now," the man said, placing himself in front of Vanning, "let's have that bag."

Vanning handed over the satchel. He looked at the man.

The man was smiling. Vanning sighed. He saw the revolver coming up and pointing at his chest. He sighed.

He said, "I knew it."

"Tough," the man said, "but that's the way it's got to be."

"Can I have a minute?"

"That's too long."

"Half a minute."

"All right."

"How about a break?"

"Don't waste time asking for a break. If you want to talk about the weather, we'll talk about the weather, but if you keep asking for a break I'll only get annoyed."

"Working for John?"

"That's right."

"Why does John use you?"

"He always uses me for this sort of thing. He doesn't like to do it himself."

"Then why didn't he use Pete?"

"Because Pete don't have a head on his shoulders. Pete has a habit of making mistakes."

"I see."

"I'm glad you see. I'm glad everything is clear."

"Except for one thing."

"Ask me, and if I can answer you I'll give you an answer."

"Why did they give me this?" Vanning said, sincere as he said it, completely naive as he took the revolver out of his pocket and showed it to the man. And the man looked at the revolver and then Vanning looked down at it and realized that it was actually a revolver and that he had it in his hand. And he looked up at the man's face and saw the dismay. And just as the dismay gave way to rage, Vanning pulled the trigger, pulled it again, then again, the shots bouncing back and forth, up and down, as the man was lowered on an invisible elevator. Vanning stepped back. Now the man was on the ground, squirming, his arms stretched out, his revolver resting near a wrist, his fingers twitching. Then his whole body twitched, gave a convulsive movement that took him over on his back, he twitched once more, his eyes opened wide, his mouth came halfway open, and he was dead.

Vanning ran. He ran as fast as he could go. There was a

hill. He ran up the hill. There was a field. He ran across the field. There was a narrow stream. He went into the stream, and the water came up to his knees, then his waist, then his chest, and he lifted one arm high, wondered why he was doing that, looked at the arm, the thing that dangled from his hand, and it was the satchel. He tried to remember picking up the satchel. He couldn't remember. But he must have picked it up. It hadn't walked into his hand. It wasn't alive. Or maybe it was. The water came up to his chin. He told himself to drop the satchel, let it sink in the stream. He told himself the bullets had hit the man, the man had fallen and dropped the satchel. And he had stood there looking at the dead man. And then he had picked up the satchel and started to run away with it.

That part of it was too much for him. He didn't have the gun. He had the satchel. He had left the gun there and had picked up the satchel. He wondered what he wanted with the satchel. He wondered why he had taken it in the first place. For that one he had an answer. He had intended to give the satchel to the police. So that was all right. But he couldn't figure out why he had taken the satchel from the dead man. Perhaps the answer was identical with the first answer. Perhaps he had still intended to visit the police. And yet that was sort of weak, because now he couldn't remember holding that idea in his mind. The only thing he now completely realized was that he had killed a man and now in his possession he had a satchel containing three hundred thousand dollars and he was running away. And he was very much afraid of the satchel.

Gradually, as his physical endurance lessened, the mental side became clearer, and he was putting pieces together and drawing conclusions. The thing that made it very bad was the way John had held the gun so close to him that people couldn't notice the gun. Even the doctor in Leadville had not seen the gun. And the hotel clerk in Denver. And the people in the lobby. Nobody had seen the gun. All they had seen was John and Pete and himself, together in the blue convertible, together in the hotel, and that made the whole thing miserable. But it had to split somewhere along the line. It couldn't keep up this way. Maybe in another ten or twenty minutes or so he would have a hold on himself and he would be ready to visit the police and tell them all about it.

The thought was in there, solid and compact, very pure and logical. But it lasted for only a few moments. After that it began to float away from him because he was telling the story to himself as he would tell it to the police, and it seemed like a foolish story. It seemed a little fantastic and more than a little ridiculous. The bathroom, for instance. They had put him in the bathroom but they had not locked the door. That was the start, and from there on it became downright comical. They had gone out of the room, leaving him in the bathroom with the door closed but unlocked. He had come out of the bathroom. And there on the bed, all ready for him, was a revolver. And there on the dresser, shining and plump was the little black satchel with all that money in it. He could see the faces of policemen, he could see them looking at each other, he could see them leaning toward him with disbelief jumping out of their eyes. And yet, with all that, one big weapon remained on his side. He still had the satchel.

He told himself that. He still had it and he could go to them and hand it over and he still had the satchel. He begged himself to believe that he still had it as he raised his hand, and looked at his hands, saw two white hands against the background of black woods. And no satchel.

There was a moment of nothing. No thought, no motion, nothing. Then an attempt to reason it out. Then the realization that he couldn't reason it out, it was too far away from him. It was away back there an hour ago, or two hours ago, miles away back there. Maybe during the minutes when he was crossing the stream. Maybe ten minutes later in these vast woods. Maybe an hour later. But there was no way of putting it on a definite basis, no way of remembering when he had let the satchel fall from his hand, or where he had let it fall.

Again Vanning saw the faces of policemen. Big pink faces that formed a circle around him, came moving in on him. And one of them was bigger than all the rest and the mouth was moving. He could hear the voice. The voice hit him, bounced back. He stumbled toward the voice and the voice hit him again.

The voice said, "You say you came out of that room and you were carrying the satchel. Is that right?"

"Yes," Vanning said.

"What were you going to do with the satchel?"

"Hand it over to you."

"All right. Then what?"

"He came in from behind me and put a gun in my back. We went out of the hotel. Then when we were on that narrow street he took the satchel away and told me it was too bad, but he was forced to do away with me."

"Then what?"

"I took the gun out of my pocket and shot him."

"Just like that?"

"Yes," Vanning said.

"What about his gun?"

"He didn't use it."

"Why not?"

"I guess he was too surprised. I guess that was the last thing he expected, my having a gun."

"Your own gun?"

"No," Vanning said, "I told you how I got it."

"Yes, you did tell us that, but I'm wondering if you expect us to believe it. Doesn't matter. We'll skip that section. We'll put you on the street with him. He's dead. You're standing there, looking down at him. And now what do you do?"

"I start running."

"Why?"

"I'm afraid."

"What's there to be afraid of? You haven't done anything wrong. You've killed a man, but you've done it in self-defense. You're in the clear. What bothers you?"

"The satchel. I saw that I had it in my hand. I couldn't remember picking it up. But there it was, in my hand."

"Well," the policeman said, "that was all right too. You still had the satchel. Why didn't you come into Denver and hand it over?"

"I was afraid. I didn't think you'd believe my story. You know the way it sounds. It's one of those stories that doesn't check."

"I'm glad you understand that," the policeman said. "It

47

makes things easier for both of us. So now we have you in those woods and you're running and still have the satchel. And what happens?"

"I don't have the satchel any more."

"It takes a jump away from you and runs away, is that it?"

"I just don't have that satchel any more," Vanning said. "I can't remember where I dropped it. I must have been in the woods for two or three hours and I couldn't have been traveling in a straight line. And the woods were thick, there was so much brush, there was a swampy section, there were a million places where I could have dropped the satchel. Can't you understand my condition? How confused I was? Try to understand. Give me any sort of a test. Please believe me."

"Sure," the policeman said. "I believe you. We all believe you. It's as simple and clear as a glass of water. You took the satchel. You ran away with it. That's what you say and that's what we believe. And that brings us to the other thing. In order to get that satchel you had to kill a man. So we've circled around and we've come back to it and honest to goodness mister, you're so far behind the eight ball that it looks like the head of a pin. It's too bad you had to go and get yourself mixed up with the wrong people. We're holding you on grand larceny and murder in the first degree."

"But I gave myself up. I came to you. I didn't have to do that."

"You didn't bring the satchel."

"I don't know where it is."

"Oh, now, why don't you cut that out?"

"I tell you I don't know where it is. I dropped it someplace. I lost it. Look, I didn't have to come here and tell you all this. I could have kept on running. But I came here."

"It's a point in your favor," the policeman said. "As a matter of fact, you have quite a few points on your side. No past record. The fact that the other man was holding a gun when you killed him. The fact that you had a legitimate occupation waiting for you in Chicago. So all that may get you some sort of a break. We may be able to work something out. Tell you what. You tell us where you've got that satchel hidden."

"I can't tell you that. I don't know where it is."

The policeman looked at the other faces and sighed. Then he looked at Vanning. His face loomed in front of Vanning as he said, "All right, you can still help yourself out a little, even if you want to be stubborn about that three hundred thousand. What you can do is plead guilty to grand larceny and murder in the second degree. That's giving you a break, bringing it down to second-degree murder, and that ought to send you up for about ten years. If you behave yourself you ought to get out in five, maybe even two or three if you're lucky."

"I won't do that," Vanning said. "I won't ruin myself. I'm an innocent man. I'm a young man and I'm not going to mess up my life."

The policeman shrugged. All the policemen shrugged. The woods shrugged and the sky shrugged. None of them especially cared. It meant nothing to them. It meant nothing to the universe with the exception of this one tiny, moving, breathing thing called Vanning, and what it meant to him was fear and fleeing. And hiding. And fleeing again. And more hiding.

He stayed in the woods for another day and another night, went on through the woods until he found a clearance, and then railroad tracks. A freight came along and he hopped it. Later he hopped another freight and still another and finally arrived in New Orleans. He called himself Wilson and got a job on the water front. The pay was good, and with time and a half for overtime he soon had enough for more travel.

In Memphis he called himself Donahue and worked as a truck driver. Then up from Memphis, a short stay in Washington and winding up in New York with three hundred dollars in his pocket. He called himself Rayburn and took the room in the Village. He went out and bought artist's materials and for two weeks he went at it furiously, building up a portfolio.

Then he went around with the portfolio and after a week of that he received his first assignment. At the beginning he had a thick mustache and wore dark glasses and combed his hair with a part in the middle. Later he discarded the glasses, and after that the mustache, and eventually he went back to the old way of combing his hair. He knew he was taking a big gamble, but it was something he had to do. He had to get rid of the hollow feeling, the grotesque knowledge that he was a hunted man.

He worked, he ate, he slept. He managed to keep going. But it was very difficult. It was almost unbearable at times, especially nights when he could see the moon from his window. He had a weakness for the moon. It gave him pain, but he wanted to see it up there. And beyond that want, so far beyond it, so futile, was the want for someone to be at his side, looking at the moon as he looked at it, sharing the moon with him. He was so lonely. And sometimes in this loneliness he became exceedingly conscious of his age, and he told himself he was missing out on the one thing he wanted above all else, a woman to love, a woman with whom he could make a home. A home. And children. He almost wept whenever he thought about it and realized how far away it was. He was crazy about kids. It was worth everything, all the struggle and heartache and worry, if only someday he could marry someone real and good, and have kids. Four kids, five kids, six kids, and grow up with them, show them how to handle a football, romp with them on the beach with their mother watching, smiling, so proudly, happily, and sitting at the table with her face across from him, and the faces of the kids, and waking up in the morning and going to work, knowing there was something to work for, and all that was as far away as the moon, and at times it seemed as though the moon was shaking its big pearly head and telling him it was no go, he might as well forget about it and stop eating his heart out.

The moon expanded after a while, and it became a brightly lit room that had two faces planted on the ceiling. One of the faces was big and wore glasses. The other face was gray and bony and topped by a balding skull. The faces flowed down from the ceiling and became stabilized, attached to torsos that stood on legs. And Vanning groaned.

Then he blinked a few times and put a hand to his mouth. The hand came away bloody. He looked at the blood. He tasted blood in his mouth.

A door opened. Vanning turned and saw John entering the room. He grinned at John.

John had his hands in trousers pockets and was biting his lip and gazing at nothing special. Vanning stood up, stumbled and hit the bed and fell on it.

Pete moved toward Vanning and John said, "No."

"Let me work on him alone," Pete said. "Sam gets in my way."

"You hit him too hard," Sam said. "You knocked him out too fast. That ain't the way."

"I don't need Sam, I can operate better alone," Pete said. He was removing brass knuckles from his right hand. He rubbed his hands together and took a step toward the bed.

"Leave him alone," John said. "Get away from him."

"I'd like a drink of water," Vanning said.

"Sure," John said. "Sam, go get him a drink of water."

Sam walked out of the room. Pete stood there, near the bed, rubbing his hands and smiling at Vanning. Quiet streamed through the room and became thick in the middle of the room. Finally John looked at Vanning.

"Hurt much?" John said.

"Inside of my mouth. Cut up."

"Lose any teeth?"

"I don't know. I don't care."

"Let me work on him alone," Pete said again.

John looked at Pete and said, "Get the hell out of here."

Pete shrugged and walked out of the room and John took a revolver from his shoulder holster and played with it for a while. He sighed a few times, frowned a few times, twisted his face as if he was trying to get a fly off it, and then he stood up and went to the wall and leaned there, looking at Vanning.

The quiet came back and settled in the center of the room. Vanning collected some blood in his mouth, spat it onto the floor. He took out a handkerchief and dabbed it against his mouth and looked at the blood, bright against white linen. He looked at John, and John was there against the wall, looking back at him, and it went on that way for several minutes, and then the door opened and Sam came in with a glass of water.

Vanning took the glass, and without looking at it he lifted it to his mouth, sent the water into his mouth, choked on the water, pegged the glass at Sam's face. The glass hit Sam

51

on the side of his face, broke there, and some glass got through Sam's flesh. Sam threw a hand inside his lapel.

"No," John said.

"Yes. Let me." Sam's eyes were blank.

"What did you put in the water?" John said.

"Nothing," Sam said.

"Salt," Vanning said. "Try tasting salt water when your mouth is all cut up."

John walked over to Sam, gestured with the revolver, and Sam walked out of the room. John turned and faced Vanning and said, "You see the way it is? They like this. They get a kick out of it. That's what you're up against. Every few minutes they'll get a new idea and they'll want to try it on you."

"I feel sorry for myself," Vanning said, "but I can't do anything about it."

"I'll let you in on something," John said. "If you think I'm enjoying this, you're crazy."

"Then why don't you stop it?"

"The cash."

"Suppose you were in my place," Vanning said. "Suppose you knew you were going to go out the hard way if you didn't talk. Would you talk?"

"Sure," John said. "I'm no fool. I'd save myself a lot of grief. Money means a lot to me, but it doesn't mean that much."

"Do you think it means that much to me?"

"I think you're sore, that's all. You're so burned up that it's got the best of you. Either that or you're one of these morons who thinks it's the trend to be brave."

"You're way off," Vanning said. "I'm too mature for the Rover Boy act. I'm too scared to be angry. And I have enough common sense to realize that eventually I'll be dead if I don't tell you where that money is. That's why it's such a rough situation. I don't know where it is and there's no way I can convince you of the fact."

John sighed again. He said, "I've been in this game a long time. I was sent up once for seven years. When they let me out I made up my mind to play level. It lasted for a while. I worked for a brewing outfit in Seattle. I met a girl. I don't remember, maybe I was happy. Anyway, my health was

52

good, I had an appetite, I hardly ever took a d.... began to see things. The way so many people let then wide open for a smart play. Even the big people. So you .... figure out what happened to me. I went back to the old game. Just jockeying around at first. A few gasoline stations, a store now and then. Then a small bank in Spokane. And then a bigger bank in Portland. Finally the important job in Seattle. And that was going to be the last transaction."

"Even this won't do you any good," Vanning said. "How can you sell me something when I'm in no position to buy?"

As if Vanning had not interrupted, John went on, "It was going to be the last. After the split and expenses, I figured on a little more than two hundred grand for myself. And then I'd wait awhile until things blew over and I'd go back to Seattle and get in touch with that girl. Look. I'll show you something."

Holding the revolver at his side, John used his other hand to extract a wallet from a hip pocket. He opened the wallet, handed it to Vanning. Under celluloid there was a picture of the girl. She was very young. Maybe she wasn't even twenty. Her hair came down in long, loose waves that played with her shoulders. She was smiling. The way her face was arranged it was easy to see that she was a little girl, and skinny, and probably not too brilliant.

Vanning handed back the wallet. He bit his lower lip in a thoughtful way and he said, "She's pretty."

"Good kid." John replaced the wallet in his pocket.

"Does she know?"

"She knows everything."

"And where does that leave her?"

"Up a tree, for the time being," John said. "But she doesn't care. She's willing to wait. And then we're going away together. You know what I always wanted? A boat."

"Fishing?"

"Just going. In a boat. I know about boats. I worked on freighters tripping back and forth between the West Coast and South America. Once I worked on a rich man's yacht. I've always wanted my own boat. That Pacific is a big hunk of water. All those islands."

"I've seen some of them."

You have?" John leaned forward. He was smiling with interest.

"Quite a few of them. But I didn't have time to concentrate on the scenery. There was too much activity taking place. And smoke got in the way."

John nodded. "I get it. But just think of working out from the West Coast with all that water to move around in. All those islands out there ahead. A forty-footer with a Diesel engine. And go from one island to another. And look at them all. No real estate agent to bother me with the build-up. Just look them over and let them give me their own build-up. And let me make my own choice."

"You wouldn't stay long."

"You don't know me."

"You don't know yourself. You'd start thinking about another bank and another three hundred thousand. You're built that way, John. It's not your fault."

"Whose fault is it?"

"Who knows? Something must have happened when you were a kid. Not enough playgrounds in your town."

John grinned. "You talk like a defense attorney. It's a funny thing. I like you. You're game. You don't make a lot of noise. You can handle yourself. Maybe I'll take you along on my boat."

"I'll be looking forward to it."

John twisted his face and stared part Vanning. "I'll bet we could actually strike up a friendship. What do I call you?"

"Jim."

"Cigarette, Jimmy?"

"Okay."

And then after the cigarettes were lit, John said, "That's what I have in mind. That boat. And you're wrong about my coming back. I'd never come back. Just that little island and the girl and me. We'd have everything two people need. Figure it out."

"That's what I'm doing," Vanning said. "And there's a piece in there that doesn't fit. The money. Why would you need all that money?"

"The boat. Supplies. General expenses. It adds up."

"It doesn't hit a couple hundred thousand. Nowhere

near that. If we made an itemized list you'd see how little you needed."

"We'll do that later," John said. "After I have the money."

Vanning hauled at the cigarette. He liked what was happening. It was giving him time, and he wanted that more than anything else. With time he could think, and with enough thinking there would be some sort of plan. Up till now the atmosphere had exhibited a completely hopeless quality. And now he had reason to think there might be a way to go on living.

"When I have that boat," John said, "I won't wait. I'll get on the boat with her and we'll shove off. Did you ever stop to think how cities crowd you? They move in on you, like stone walls moving in. You get the feeling you'll be crushed. It happens slow, but you imagine it happens fast. You feel like yelling. You want to run. You don't know where to run. You think if you start running something will stop you."

"I don't mind cities," Vanning said.

"Cities hurt my eyes. I don't like the country, either. I like the water. I know once I get on that water, going across it, going away, I'll be all right. I won't be nervous any more."

"You don't seem nervous."

"My nerves are in bad shape," John said. "I have a devil of a time falling asleep. How do you sleep?"

"The past eight months haven't been so good."

"You'll sleep fine after we get this deal cleared up."

"I guess so."

"How about it, Jimmy?"

Vanning squeezed the cigarette, watched the burning end detach itself from unlit tobacco, watched shreds of tobacco dripping from the paper shell. Emotion became an unknown thing, replaced now by curiosity. He wanted John to go on talking. He wanted an explanation of that sequence in Denver, the peculiar combination of revolver and satchel and empty room. But he couldn't ask about that. If he did ask, and if John gave him an answer, he would be strangely obligated to John, and he couldn't afford to be placed in that position. He had nothing to offer in return.

"I'm thinking about it," he said.

"That's fine," John said, and there was a faint touch of desperation in his voice. "You go on thinking about it. Don't worry about it. Just give it some thought. We'll figure out something."

They traded smiles, and John went on talking about the boat. He got to talking about boats in general. He seemed to know his boats. They stayed with the boats for a while and then they gradually came back to the business at hand.

"Funny," John said, "how we spotted you tonight."

"It was funny and it was clever."

"Why clever?"

"The girl," Vanning said.

"What girl?"

"Come on," Vanning said, and his heart climbed to the top of a diving platform and waited there.

"Oh," John said. "That girl. That girl in the restaurant. I didn't get a good look at her. What about her?"

"That's the point," Vanning said. "What about her?"

"You ought to know."

"All I know is, she couldn't have worked it better. I'm not the smartest man around by a long shot, but I don't get fooled like that very often."

John laughed. "You're nowhere near it," he said. "She wasn't working with us. We never saw her before."

"I don't see why you're trying to save her face."

"Maybe you'll want to see her again. Maybe you like her."

"Crazy about her," Vanning said. "Why shouldn't I be? Look at all she's done for me. I ought to buy her a box of orchids."

"You make it sound as if it's important."

"It's important because it's one of those things that makes a man want to kick himself. Bad enough that I talked to her in the first place. What hurts the most is that I let her take me down a street with only one small light on it."

"Maybe it's all for the best," John said. "Now we'll get the whole thing straightened out and everything will be fine."

"And dandy. Don't forget the dandy."

"Fine and dandy," John said, and he grinned, and then he stopped grinning.

Because Vanning was in there, too close to him, and Vanning was moving, Vanning's hand sliding out, going toward the revolver, veering away from the revolver as it came up, closing over John's wrist. And Vanning twisted John's wrist, twisted hard, and the revolver flew out of John's hand as Vanning twisted again. Then Vanning chopped a short right that caught John on the side of the head. As John tried to straighten, Vanning clipped him again, and a third time, and John was going down, hitting the edge of the bed, trying to get up.

Vanning allowed him to get halfway up, allowed him to start opening his mouth. Then Vanning reached back, hardened his right hand, sent it in on a straight line, direct and clean and exploding. John's eyes closed and John sagged, reached the floor, rolled over and stayed there.

Vanning stepped to the window and looked down. There was a ledge a few feet below. He climbed out of the window and placed himself on the ledge, looked down, saw another ledge, descended to that as he noticed the way the porch roof was placed. He was going down. Hanging from fingertips, he worked his way to a spot reasonably close to the porch roof, then let go. He didn't make much noise as he hit the porch roof, but it seemed like thunder. He waited there, and the echo of the thunder passed away and there was no more noise. He jumped from the porch roof, and he was wondering if they had left the ignition keys in the green sedan.

Chapter Six

There was another ferryboat, much larger than the first one. And the big wave was moving in again. Fraser opened his eyes, twisted his head and saw a gleam of gray-lavender slicing through the venetian blinds. He rolled over and got out of bed, and immediately his wife was awake and sitting up.

"I'm getting dressed" Fraser said.

"So early?"

"I shouldn't have left him last night."

57

"Get back in bed."

"No," he said. "I've got to make sure." He moved toward the dresser. He opened a drawer and took out a tan leather case with a long strap attached to it. He dressed quickly, slung the strap over his shoulder, and he looked as though he was headed for the races at Jamaica.

"Breakfast?" she said.

"No, I don't have time."

"A glass of orange juice?"

"No," he said. "Thanks, honey, but this is on the double."

"Call me," she said. "I want to know."

He nodded and hurried out of the room. He was impatient in the elevator and more impatient on the street that was quite empty and especially empty in regard to taxis. He had to walk a block before he spotted one.

The taxi took him down to Greenwich Village, stopped a half block away from where he wanted to go. He walked quickly the rest of the way, entered a house across the street from Vanning's place, ran up to the room he had rented for the purpose of watching Vanning's room. He opened the leather case and took out a pair of binoculars.

At the window he held the binoculars to his eyes and focused on Vanning's room. He saw the empty room and a bed that had not been slept in. He stood there at the window with the binoculars against his eyes and the empty room looked back.

He put the binoculars back in the case. They were wonderful binoculars. They had cost plenty and if they weren't so valuable he would have kept them in this room, but the house was a shabby place and some of these tenants had a habit of visiting other rooms by means of a skeleton key. Now, however, he didn't particularly care if someone took the binoculars. He left the case on a table and walked out of the room.

There was a need for talking to someone, and Fraser decided to call Headquarters. Downstairs there was a pay phone, and he inserted a coin, moved his hand toward the dial, discovered that he was not calling Headquarters, but his wife. She must have been sitting near the phone and waiting for the call, because she answered at once.

"He's gone," Fraser said.

58

"Are you sure?"

"I tell you he's gone."

"Please don't get excited."

"I've ruined it."

"Please—"

"I was too sure of myself. When I left him last night I could have sworn he'd head for his room and go to sleep. He'd been working at his board. He had an appointment today with an art director. I had it all checked. I was so sure. I'm gifted that way, I always know what I'm doing. I'm terrific—"

"Now cut it out, will you?"

"I think I'll resign—"

"Stop it. Come on home—"

"No," Fraser said. "I feel like taking a walk. I know where there's a grammar school around here. I think I'll enroll in kindergarten."

"Stay there. Maybe he'll come back."

"No, he's gone."

"I said stay there."

"Do you still like me?"

"Yes."

"Do you?" he asked. "Really?"

"Yes, dear."

"I don't think there's much to like. I shouldn't be giving you my troubles."

"If you didn't I wouldn't like you. But do you want me to like you a great deal?"

"Yes," Fraser said, "I want you to like me very much."

"Then stay there."

"He won't come back."

"Maybe he will. Please stay there."

"What for?"

"There's a chance—"

"I don't think so. I think they got him."

"Who?"

"Those other men. It's the first time he hasn't come home. What other kind of work do you think I'm fitted for?"

"I'm getting very angry at you."

"Maybe I'll go down to Headquarters."

"I don't want you to do that."

"I've got to go down there. I've got to tell them. Tell them now. Get it over with. Get the whole goddamn thing over with. I'm going down—"

"No—"

"See you later—"

"I said no. Stay on the phone. Don't you hang up—"

"Why?"

"I want to talk to you."

"What about?"

"Us."

"You and me?"

"And the kids," she said.

"All right, talk. I'll listen."

"I have faith in you," she said. "You're the finest man I've ever known. Sometimes I feel like walking up to strangers and telling them all about my husband. And the kids are so proud of you. And I'm so proud—"

"You ought to see me now."

"Does it mean anything when I say I have faith in you?"

"It makes me feel worse," he said. His voice was very low. He had lived a fairly quiet life, considering the field he was in, and aside from the technical excitement and ups and downs he had suffered no more disappointments and setbacks than the average man. He had been able to take all that without too much grief or self-dislike, but now he was extremely despondent and he was rather close to hating himself. Not for what he had done to himself, but the connection between the ruin of his career and the future of his wife and children. He had a feeling that right at this point his family was very insecure. And not because Headquarters would kick him out. They wouldn't kick him out. He had been with them too long. His record was excellent.

That was it. His record was much too excellent. They'd pat him on the back and tell him to forget all about this one. They'd tell him to take a week off and get a rest and come back refreshed. But he wouldn't come back that way. He would come back with the rigid, icy knowledge that he was going downhill. And already he was descending. The moment he walked into Headquarters to report this matter, he would be going downward at a terrific rate, with no support or elevation in sight. And that was what he had to do. He had to tell Headquarters about this, and immediately.

"I've got to hang up now," he said. "I'm going to Headquarters."

"Will you do something for me?" There was a desperation in her voice and it was as though she had seen inside his mind. "Will you wait there another hour? Just give it another hour. Please, for me."

"That's against regulations. We've got to report these things right away."

"I'm asking you to gamble."

"High stakes," he said. And he meant it. Despite his record, despite his many years on the job, he couldn't defy routine procedure without taking the risk of being fired. Even though they liked him very much, they had a habit of taking this sort of thing quite seriously. Maybe they would throw him out, after all, just to set an example.

"I know it's taking a big chance," she said. "But do it anyway, for me."

He bit at the inside of his mouth. "An hour?"

"Just an hour."

There was an odd certainty in her voice. He had to smile. It was a strained, weary smile. "You're selling me something," he said. "You want me to think you're clairvoyant."

"Promise me you'll stay there an hour."

He waited for several moments, and then he said, "All right."

"You promise? Really?"

"Yes."

And he put the receiver back on the hook. He walked up the dusty stairway, went into the room. He picked up the binoculars and moved toward the window.

Chapter Seven

There was morning gray in the sky as the sedan crossed Brooklyn Bridge. There was some pale blue in the sky as Vanning parked the car in an alleyway off Canal Street. He used the subway to get back to the Village, and upon entering his room the first direct move he made was to start packing his things. After some minutes of that he changed his mind, sat on a chair near the window and smoked cigarettes while he toyed with various angles. He was certain they didn't know his address. He told himself not to be too certain of anything. The logical step at this point was something simple, something easy. And the easiest thing he could think of was sleep.

He slept until late afternoon, showered and shaved, concluded after a mirror inspection that he looked just a little too banged up for an appearance at the advertising agency where his illustrations were due. After breakfast, he used the restaurant phone booth, told the agency art director that he was sick with an upset stomach. The art director told him tomorrow would be all right, joked with him about the effects of alcohol on a man's stomach, told him milk was the best medicine for a raw stomach. Vanning thanked the agency man and hung up. He took a subway uptown. He didn't know where he was going. He wanted to get away from the Village. He wanted to think.

It kept jabbing away at him, the desire to get out of this city, to travel and keep on traveling. But it wasn't traveling. It was running. And the desire was curtained by the knowledge that running was a move without sensible foundation. Retreat was only another form of waiting. And he was sick of waiting. There had to be some sort of accomplishment, and the only way he could accomplish anything was to move forward on an offensive basis.

He was part of a crowd on Madison Avenue in the Seventies, and he was swimming through schemes, discarding one after another. The schemes moved off indifferently as he pushed them away. He walked into a drugstore and ordered a dish of orange ice. Sitting there, with the orange ice in front of him, he picked up a spoon, tapped it against his palm, told himself to take it from the beginning and pick up the blocks one by one and see if he could build something.

There weren't many blocks. There was John. There was Pete and there was Sam. There was a green sedan. There was the house on the outskirts of Brooklyn. None of those was any good. There was the man who had died in Denver.

And that was no good. There was Denver itself. There were the police in Denver. The police.

A voice said, "You want to eat that orange ice or drink it?"

Vanning looked up and saw the expressionless face of a soda clerk.

"It's melting," the soda clerk said.

"Melting," Vanning said.

"Sure. Can't you see?"

"Tell me something," Vanning said.

"Anything. I'm a whiz."

"I'll bet you are. I'll bet you know everything there is to know about orange ice."

"People, too."

"Let's stay with the orange ice."

"Whatever you say. It's no longer a sellers' market. Nowadays we've got to please the customers.

"It doesn't take much to please me," Vanning said. "I'm just curious about this orange ice."

"No mosquitoes in it. We spray the stuff every day."

"I mean the way it melts."

"It don't melt in winter, mister. But this is summer. It's hot in summer. That's why the ice melts. Okay?"

"Okay for a start. But let's go on from there."

"Sure. Just as soon as I fix a black-and-white for Miss America down there."

Vanning waited. He dipped the spoon into the melting pale orange dome and left it there. The soda clerk came back and said, "Now where were we?"

"The orange ice. Look, it's nearly all melted."

"That's the way things go. It's a tough world."

"But suppose we use our heads about this. Suppose we freeze it again. What I'm driving at is, a thing may look ruined, but if you give it a certain treatment you can bring it back to normal. You can still use it."

"That's what I claim," the soda clerk said. "Never say die. Someday I'll own Manhattan. Just watch my speed."

" Good for you," Vanning said. He picked up the check, put a fifty-cent piece on the counter and walked toward the telephone booths. There was a buzzing in his mind and it was a healthy buzzing. He liked the feel of it, the soundless sound of it. He entered a booth, closed the door, took some change out of his pocket.

He put a coin in the slot.

"Number, please?"

"I want to call Denver."

"What is that, sir?"

"Denver, Colorado."

"What number, sir?"

"Police headquarters."

"Station to station?"

"That's right, and don't cut in on me. I'll signal when I'm finished."

"Just a moment, sir."

He waited several moments. Then the operator waited while Vanning left the booth and got the necessary change. She was arranging the connection for him, he was putting quarters and dimes into the slots, he was waiting.

And then he heard her saying "New York calling. Just a moment, please."

A voice said, "Yes? Hello?"

Vanning leaned toward the mouthpiece. "Is this police headquarters in Denver?"

"That's right. Who is this?"

Vanning gave the name of a New York newspaper. He said, "Features department. This is Mr. Rayburn, associate editor. I'm wondering if you could help me out."

"Just a minute."

The voice handed him over to another voice. And then a third voice. And a fourth.

The fourth voice said, "All right, what can we do for you?"

"May I know whom I'm speaking to?"

"Hansen. Homicide. What's on your mind?"

Vanning repeated the self-introduction he had given to the first voice. He said, "We'd like to do a feature story on a murder that took place in Denver some time ago."

"That's not telling me much."

"Eight months ago."

"Solved?"

"That's what we don't know. We got the shreds of it from hearsay."

"Any names?"

"No," Vanning said. "That's why I'm calling. We don't have any record of it in our files. But from what we've picked up, it's one of the sensational things."

"Is that all you can tell me?"

Vanning stared at the wall beyond the telephone and told himself to hang up. This was a crazy move. It was packed chock-full of risk. If he stayed on the phone too long, if he made one slip they would trace the call. Maybe they were tracing it already. He couldn't understand why he was staying on the phone. For a moment he wanted them to trace the call, he wanted them to nab him, once and for all, get the entire affair over with, one way or another. In the following moment he told himself to hang up and walk out of the drugstore and leave the neighborhood. But something kept him attached to the phone. He didn't know what it was. His mind was filled with an assortment of jugglers and they were dropping Indian pins all over the place.

He said, "We know the victim was a man. The killer was identified, but he got away."

"Wait a minute. I'll have a look at the files."

Vanning lit a cigarette. The quiet phone was like an ocean without waves. He blew smoke into the mouthpiece and watched it radiate. The minute went by. Another minute went by. And a third. And a fourth. The operator was in there for a few seconds, and Vanning told her to come in at the end of the call and tell him what he owed the phone company. Then the phone was quiet again. And another minute went by.

And then the voice from Denver went on again, saying "Maybe this is it. You there?"

"I'm listening."

"Eight months ago. A man named Harrison. Shot and killed a few blocks away from the Harlan Hotel. Suspect a man named James Vanning. Still at large."

"That's it."

"What about it?"

"Can you give me anything?"

"Nothing you could build into a story. But then again I'm not in the newspaper business."

"Anything at all."

"Listen if it's this important, why don't you send a man down?"

"We will, if I think the thing can be shaped into something."

"I doubt it, but you'll be paying good money for the call. You want to take it down?"

"I'm ready. Shoot."

"Harrison, Fred. Record of six arrests. Served time for robbery. Arrested on a murder charge in 1936 but case thrown out of court for lack of evidence. On probation at time he was murdered. From there on we're in the dark. No motive. No trace of the suspect."

"You sure about your suspect?"

"No doubt about it. Fingerprints on the gun. Vanning's car parked near the Harlan Hotel. Vanning registered at the Harlan Hotel under the name of Dilks, along with two other men.

"Their names?"

"Smith and Jones. You can see what we have to work with."

"Anything more on Vanning?"

"He was spotted with Harrison in the lobby of the hotel. About ten minutes before the murder. Someone piped them leaving the hotel together. That was the last time he was seen."

"Try to stay with him," Vanning said. "I don't promise anything definite, but we may be able to dig up a few facts you can use. Try to give me more on the man."

"There isn't much to give. On the face of it, we'd say that the job was handled by a hired killer. But this Vanning keeps us guessing. No record of past arrests. Worked as a commercial artist in Chicago. Served as a lieutenant, senior grade, in the Navy. Damage-control officer on a battleship. Silver Star. Excellent record. No past connection with victim. It's an upside-down case. We know he did it, but that's all. You said you could hand us a few facts."

"We may have something for you. Say in a few days. We're not sure yet, but there's an interesting connection that has possibilities."

"Why not let me have it now?"

"I don't want to make a fool of myself. It may not mean

anything. I don't want to lose my job. Remember, I'm only an associate editor. There's a boss over me."

"Let me speak to the boss. I'll hold the phone."

"Wait," Vanning said. "Let's see what I can do with this." He turned his face away from the mouthpiece, said to empty air, "Johnny, is the boss around?" Then he waited. Then he came back to the mouthpiece and said, "Wait there a minute."

"I'm waiting."

Vanning lit another cigarette, took small, rapid puffs at it, closed his eyes, his forehead deeply creased in groping thought. All at once he snapped his fingers. The idea was glaring and he didn't see any holes in it. He whipped out his breast-pocket handkerchief, put it across the mouthpiece, put his voice on a high-pitched, nasal plane as he said, "Callahan speaking. Features editor."

"This is Hansen. Denver police. Homicide department."

"What did Rayburn tell you?"

"Nothing. He only asked questions. But he said he might be able to tell me something. He said it was a little over his head, so I asked if I could speak with you."

"If Rayburn was a good newspaperman, he wouldn't be dragging me in here. I don't know why they're always putting these things on my shoulders."

"Look, Callahan, that's between you and Rayburn. I'm a policeman and we're trying to catch a murderer. You're trying to get a story. If we can help each other out, that's fine. But you can't expect me to throw information your way and have you sit there in New York and hold back on me. If you have something you think we can use, let's have it. Otherwise, stop wasting your time and mine."

"I guess you make sense."

"I guess I do."

"Okay," Vanning said. "I'll give it to you but I want you to understand it's not a definite lead. It's just something we picked up more or less by accident. Some character called us up and told us a story about a bank robbery in Seattle. About eight or nine months ago, he said it was. A big job, three hundred thousand dollars. He said it was connected with a murder in Denver. We called Seattle and they told us the bank robbers were traced as far as Colorado."

67

"That's interesting."

"Is it new to you?"

"Brand-new. Tell me something. How many men were in on that Seattle thing?"

"Three," Vanning said, and he tried to bite it back before it hit the mouthpiece, but it was already in the mouthpiece, it was already in Denver.

"Three men. That adds up to Dilks and Smith and Jones. That brings Vanning in on the bank job. I'm going to check with Seattle. I think you've handed us something we can use. Will you hold the phone a minute?"

"Don't be too long," Vanning said.

He took a deep breath, blew it out toward the handkerchief spread and tightened across the telephone mouthpiece. He wondered how long he had been in the phone booth. It seemed as if he had been here for a full day. And it seemed as if he was making one mistake after another. There were too many things to remember, and already he had forgotten one of the most important, that angle concerning Sam, the fact that Sam had been absent from the Denver affair. Sam had been in Leadville, under the care of that doctor. Three men in the Seattle robbery. Three men in the Denver deal. He felt like rapping himself in the mouth. Now he had gone and done it. Now he was glued to Seattle as well as Denver. Now he had taken Sam's place in the line-up. He was only a substitute and yet at the same time he was the headline performer. He was the star, the stellar attraction, he was the goat, the ignoramus who deserved every rotten break he got. This phone call was just another major error in a long parade of major errors. He was kidding himself now and he had been kidding himself all along. He wasn't a criminal, he wasn't even an amateur criminal. He was a commercial artist, a grown man, an ordinary citizen who believed in law and order, a man who looked upon too much excitement as an unnatural, neurotic thing. He didn't belong in this muddle, this circle, that went round and round much too fast.

The voice from Denver was there again. "Hello. Callahan?"

"Still here."

"We're checking with Seattle. Can you hold on?"

"I'll wait."

"Good. We won't be long."

Vanning put another cigarette in his mouth, had no desire to light it. He put his hand in front of his eyes, wondered why his fingers weren't shaking. Perhaps he had gone beyond that. Perhaps it was actually a bad sign, his steady fingers. He sat there, his head lowered, feeling sorry for himself, sorry for every poor devil who had ever stumbled into a spot like this. And then, gradually lifting his head, he gradually smiled. It was such a miserable state of affairs that it was almost comical. If people could see him now their reactions would be mixed. Some of them would have pity for him. Others would smile as he was smiling at this moment. Maybe some of them would laugh at him, as they would laugh at Charlie Chaplin in hot water somewhere up in the Klondike.

He sighed. He thought of other men, thousands of them, hundreds of thousands, working in factories, in offices, and going back tonight to a home-cooked meal, sitting in parlors with their wives and kids, listening to Bob Hope, going to sleep at a decent hour, and really sleeping, with nothing to anticipate except another day of work and another evening at home with the family. That was all they looked forward to, and Vanning told himself he would give his right arm if that was all he could look forward to.

"Callahan?"

"Yes?"

"Just stay there. Be with you in a jiffy. We're still talking to Seattle on another phone."

"Make it snappy, will you?"

"Be right with you."

Vanning struck a match and applied it to the cigarette that waited in his mouth. He took in some smoke blew it out, turned his head and saw a girl waiting outside the phone booth. She seemed to be fed up with waiting, and her pose was typical, the hand on the hip, the head tilted to one side, the lips tightened sarcastically and saying, Go on, take all day, it's so silly to consider other people. He smiled sheepishly, and her expression changed, she glared at him. She looked very attractive, glaring. Pretty girl with an upsweep, pretty and slim and extremely Madison Avenue.

It was getting on toward the cocktail hour and evidently she wanted to check on her date at Theodore's or the Drake and it was a shame he had to keep her waiting like this. It was really unfair. All she wanted to do was keep that date, and all he wanted to do was keep himself alive. Now her expression had changed again and she seemed really worried about getting to the phone. He was just a little annoyed at himself, because he was getting an eerie sort of satisfaction watching her frown in worriment. At least he wasn't the only worried individual in this world.

The girl shifted her position, breathed in and out in an exasperated way.

Vanning opened the booth door, leaned out and said, "I'm calling Denver."

"How lovely."

"I'm awfully sorry it's taking this long."

"We're both sorry."

"Maybe one of the other booths—"

"No, darling. Everybody's calling Denver."

"I'll try to rush it."

"Please do. I want to break the date before he gets there."

"I thought you wanted to keep the date," Vanning said.

"I want to break it. I hope you don't mind."

"It depends. Maybe he's a nice guy.

"He's very unexciting," the girl said. "He wants to get married. What are you doing with that handkerchief over the mouthpiece?"

"I have a cold. I don't want anyone else to get it. I—"

Denver was in again. Vanning closed the door, came back to the mouthpiece.

The voice was saying, "I think you've started something, Callahan. We have Seattle all worked up. They tell us three men did that bank job. Got away in a phaeton. Two men in the bank and one waiting in the car. One of the men was big. Hefty around the chest and shoulders. Wore a felt hat and a loafer jacket with a wide collar turned up. That was probably Vanning, alias Dilks. Now we're going to check with the Navy to see when he got out. The way we have it lined up, Harrison was waiting in Denver, acting as contact man. There must have been an argument over the split, and Vanning pulled a gun and that's about as close as we can come to it right now. That character you were telling us about, if he calls up again see if you can meet him somewhere. See if you can hold him down. And listen, if anything new turns up, get in touch with us, will you?"

"By all means."

"And thanks for the tip."

"I'm thanking you," Vanning said. "I think we'll have a swell story."

"You bet. 'Bye now." And the other party hung up.

The operator asked for more money and Vanning paid it. He put the handkerchief back in his pocket, and as he left the phone booth the girl went whizzing in to take his place. He walked through the drugstore, arranged his lips to whistle a tune, couldn't get the tune past his lips.

On Madison Avenue again, he waved to a cab, climbed in and fell back against leather-looking upholstery, and the cab started south on Madison.

"Where to?"

"Fifth Avenue and Eighth Street."

"You in a hurry?"

"No," Vanning said. "Why?"

"Just wondered."

Vanning closed his eyes, slumped in the seat, stayed that way for several seconds and then slowly opened his eyes and gazed at the driver's head. There was considerable traffic in front of the taxi's windshield, but Vanning didn't see it. He was studying the driver's head. The driver wore a cloth cap. The driver had recently treated himself to a haircut. The barber was either a newcomer to the trade or not too much interested in the work. It was a very bad haircut.

The taxi made a turn, made another turn and came onto Fifth Avenue.

The haircut was bad because it took too much hair from the driver's skull, and instead of shading gradually from hair to shaven neck, it broke up acutely, so that there was a distinct cleavage between black hair and white flesh. That was one thing that made the driver seem a little wrong. And another thing was the way the driver sat at the wheel. The driver leaned to one side, and didn't seem to be watching the traffic in front. Instead, the driver seemed to aim attention at the rearview mirror.

"Where did you get that haircut?" Vanning said.

"What's the matter with it?"

"Everything."

"Makes no difference," the driver said. "Who sees me?"

"Don't you care how you look?"

"All I care about is getting rid of hair in the summer. If men had any sense, they'd shave their entire heads. Nothing like it if you want to keep cool."

The taxi made another turn. It was going toward Sixth Avenue.

"Why not stay on Fifth?"

"Too much traffic."

"I'm a New Yorker," Vanning said. "Just as much traffic on Sixth. Just as many lights."

"Should we try Eighth?"

"That's taking me out of my way."

"You said you weren't in a hurry."

Vanning leaned forward. "That's what I said. That's why I'm wondering why we didn't stay on Fifth."

"You want me to cut off the meter? I don't need the money. I make out."

The taxi passed Sixth Avenue, passed Broadway, moved on toward Eighth.

"Sure," the driver said. "I break even. I don't have to stretch a ride. I never go in for that sort of thing. And I don't like to be accused of it, either. I been driving a cab for fifteen years and I never stretched a ride. I like when people start telling me how to operate a cab."

"What do you want me to do, sit here and argue with you?"

"I like when these people think they're doing me a favor when they get in the cab. I got more money in the bank than most of the people who ride with me. And you don't have to tip me if you don't want to. I'm not asking for a tip. I don't want anybody to think they're doing me favors."

"Now we're passing Eighth," Vanning said. "If this is a sight-seeing tour, why not start with Grant's Tomb?"

"You want me to stop the cab?" the driver said. "You can get out here if you want to."

"It sounds like an idea."

"We'll stop right here," the driver said.

The taxi slowed down, going toward the curb. The driver turned around and stared at Vanning as Vanning looked at the meter. The driver stared past Vanning. And Vanning was taking money from his pocket and then he was looking at the driver, whose eyes remained focused on the rear window.

"All right," Vanning said. "Let's forget the beef. Let's keep going."

"Maybe you better get out here."

"Keep going," Vanning said.

"It's got to be level. I can't do it if it ain't level. You know how it is."

"I said keep going."

The taxi moved away from the curb, stopped for a red light. The light changed. Traffic was thinning out. Vanning folded his arms, sat stiffly on the edge of the seat.

"Down Ninth Avenue?" the driver asked.

"Try Tenth."

"A lot of trucks on Tenth."

"All right. Ninth. Give her some speed."

"Now look, mister—"

"You heard me."

The taxi commenced racing down Ninth Avenue. A red light showed and the taxi ignored it, raced toward the next red light.

"Make a turn," Vanning said. "Turn left."

"Can't do that. One-way street. We'll be bucking traffic."

"Make the turn," Vanning said.

The taxi started a turn, veered away to remain on Ninth Avenue, cut past the next red light, then turned down a side street, and there was the sound of a policeman's whistle, and the taxi raced on.

"Back to Fifth," Vanning said." Go past Fifth. Go toward the river. Don't stop for anything."

"It ain't no good," the driver said. "We're in the center of Manhattan. We don't have no room to move. First thing you know, we'll have a smash-up. It's bound to happen."

"Don't look back at me. Keep your eyes on the windshield. Keep us moving."

"If I stop in heavy traffic you can hop out and—"

"Don't tell me how to plan my day," Vanning said. "Just

drive your taxicab and let's see if we can do something smart."

"I sure did something smart when I picked you up."

"Drive, Admiral. Just drive."

They were going past Sixth. Past Fifth. There was another red light. They went past it. They went rushing toward the rear of a huge truck, and the truck came to a stop, and the truck became an expanse of dull green wall in front of them.

"On the sidewalk," Vanning said.

Two wheels of the cab climbed up on the sidewalk, stayed on the sidewalk as the cab fought to get free. A man appeared in front of the cab, and the man's eyes bulged, the man leaped toward the wall of a building. The cab returned to the street, went tearing its way past the red light that showed on Madison.

"I needed this," the driver complained.

"Don't worry," Vanning said. "Everything's going to be all right. We're doing great."

"I'm glad you think so. That makes me feel a lot better."

Another truck blocked them off on Lexington Avenue. The driver twisted the wheel, they cut between two other cars, and the two other cars came together and there was the sound of a crash. Vanning's cab continued on its way, and in the distance there was the sound of a policeman's whistle. And another whistle.

"You hear that?" the driver said.

"I heard it."

"But that's the law."

"That's why it sounds so good."

"You don't get me, mister. I said the law. I'm doing the best I can, but we're working in a crowded city and there's too much law and not enough space. They're going to catch this cab."

"And the car in back of us."

"You know who's in back of us, mister?"

"Sure," Vanning said. "A green sedan. Right?"

"Wrong," the driver said. "Take a look. See for yourself."

Vanning stared at the driver's third-rate haircut. Then very slowly he turned and looked through the rear window and he saw another cab. It was quite a distance behind, and some cars were in front of it, but it was pushing its way past the cars. It was coming on.

"The cab?" Vanning said.

"Of course it's the cab. I thought you knew from the beginning."

"When was the beginning?"

"When you climbed in. When we started out on Madison. I saw him making a beeline for that other cab. That's why we took the long ride. I was trying to help you out."

Vaning smashed a fist into his other hand. "It's John," he said. "It's got to be John. It's got to end here. They've got to catch me and they've got to catch John. This is the windup. The only way it could end." He knew he was getting onto the hysterical side, but there was nothing he could do about it. His voice sounded odd as he said, "You hear me?"

"I hear you, mister, but I don't know what you're talking about."

"I'm talking about a bank robber named John."

"In that other cab?"

"Right."

"Wrong" the driver said. "The guy in that other cab is no bank robber. I know what he is."

"What?"

"Detective."

At first it didn't click. It was too far away. Too high up or too far underground, and Vanning had to close his eyes and rub his palms into his eyes, and then he had to take himself back, to the phone booth in the drugstore, and he had to remember how long he had stayed on the phone, talking to Denver, and he had to estimate how long it would take Denver to trace the call, how long it would take Denver to call Manhattan police, how long it would take Headquarters in Manhattan to send a man to the drugstore. Vanning figured out in terms of minutes, and then he shook his head in a convulsive way, he tried to forget that he was in a racing taxi. And just then the whole thing clicked, and it made a tremendous noise in his head. And it was too much for him.

"Take me to the river," he said. "I may as well jump in."

"Don't go nuts on me," the driver said. "Past Second Avenue I'll drive up an alley and you can hop out. We got a nice lead."

"How do you know he's a detective?"

"I've seen him around."

"You sure?"

"I'm telling you he's a plain-clothes man. I've seen him operate. What I ought to do is mind my own business. But you looked all right. You looked like a guy who needed a break."

"Where's that alley?"

"Not far," the driver said. "From now on," he promised, "I'll get my excitement in the movies."

"Drive," Vanning said. "I'm an innocent man. Believe me—"

Slashing past Second Avenue, the cab almost made contact with another truck, curved away, and then out in front of the truck, then past a jalopy, then made a turn into a wide alleyway. On one side there was a gate that ran the length of the alley, and beyond the gate a grim line of wall with no windows showing. On the other side there was a warehouse, and Vanning saw windows and he saw doorways, and a few of the doors were open.

His wallet was out, he was flipping a twenty-dollar bill toward the front seat, the cab was coming to a stop.

"Keep moving," he said. "Drive up the alley. After that I don't care what you do."

He jerked the door handle, leaped out of the cab, sprinted across the alley and threw himself at the nearest open doorway. As he went in, he could hear the noise made by an approaching siren.

The warehouse was a huge place. It was quite dark in the area across which Vanning moved. He had to move slowly because it was so dark. Men's voices came from somewhere on the floor above. Vanning walked into a column of boxes, grabbed them as they started to topple over.

"Charlie Chaplin again," he murmured. "Come on, you. Cut out the comedy."

But he was having trouble getting the boxes back in place, and they were large boxes and they almost knocked him over. He knew he was grinning. And as he kept on grinning he became a little afraid of it. To grin at a time like this was all wrong, unreasonable. And the wrongness of it harmonized with all the other wrong stunts he had pulled.

The absurd phone call to Denver. He couldn't get his finger on the exact reason why he had called Denver. Maybe because he wanted to find out how much they knew. Maybe because he wanted to throw some bait their way in the hope of making a bargain. Just what kind of bargain he had figured on making he couldn't remember. There had to be a trickle of logic in it somewhere, but now, at this special juncture, he saw the phone call as an extremely foolish thing.

And those other foolish things. Assuming that the car behind the cab had been a green sedan with John and Pete and Sam in it. So very sure that it had been a green sedan, failing to remember that he had taken the green sedan on a ride from the outskirts of Brooklyn. Now he remembered the ride but he couldn't remember the geography of the ride, he couldn't remember the location of the house where they had negotiated with him. Not even the approximate location of the house. And he couldn't remember where he had parked the green sedan. Somewhere near the subway station on Canal Street, but that was no good. There were too many streets, too many alleys near the Canal Street subway. And all this harmony of error was harmonizing with that first tremendous error, that satchel business, and it didn't get him anywhere to tell himself he was absent-minded. Lapse of memory might be good for a laugh in a courtroom, but bad otherwise.

All this was saddening, it was downhill. Vanning begged himself to get away from the negative side. Too much of it would lead to complete fear, and if he ever reached that point he might just as well take gas. Defeat was a whirl-pool, and the only thing to do was swim away from it, keep swimming, no matter how strong the downward drag. He still had his life, he still had his health, his brain had stalled several times but it was still a brain, it still functioned.

And now it told him there was no such thing as a super-human being, and even Babe Ruth had suffered a batting slump every now and then, and even Hannibal had undergone military setbacks, even Einstein had flunked in mathematics on one amazing occasion. And then there was another way to look at it.

Gravity was a powerful thing, but someone had invented the parachute. Oceans had tremendous depths, and yet someone had invented a vessel that would go down and down and then come up again and reach the surface. Vanning told himself to invent an idea that would get him clear of the downhill path and bring him up. It was time for that. He had gone down far enough, too far. It was time to start climbing. It was time to stop the foolish grin and the relaxed submission to all the leering goblins.

He walked through the warehouse. There was a door leading out to air and sunlight. There were some men standing near the door. A few were in their shirtsleeves. Others wore overalls. A husky man wearing a cap and smoking a cigar was loudly enthusiastic over a new welterweight from Minneapolis. Vanning walked toward the group. They blocked his path to the door. They turned and looked at him. He stared at them as he approached. He stared past them, indicating that he intended leaving the warehouse. They continued to block the door. They all looked at him.

"Going out," Vanning said.

The big man with the cigar was lowering the cigar from tobacco-stained lips. "You connected here?"

"City inspector," Vanning said.

"Inspecting what?"

"Plumbing."

"How we doing?"

"Water's still running," Vanning said. "That's good enough."

The big man stepped out of Vanning's way. And Vanning walked through the doorway. Adding distance between himself and the warehouse, he moved on toward First Avenue. He walked fast on First Avenue, watching the street, looking for a cab. There was slightly less than five minutes of this, and then a cab, and then a slow ride downtown, a few cigarettes, and then a short stroll across part of Washington Square, and finally his apartment.

He took off his coat, seated himself near the window. He sat there doing nothing for quite a while. Heat came up from the Village pavements and threw itself against him. He picked himself up from the chair, walked to the kitchenette, opened the refrigerator. Busy with bottles and ice, he anticipated his drink and enjoyed the idea that he was doing something constructive. He mixed a third of scotch with two thirds of soda, used a good deal of ice, took the glass back to the window, sat down and took his time with the drink.

Three drinks later he was in a fairly comfortable frame of mind. He looked out and saw the sky taking on a blend of orange and purple, lighting up in the fierce, frantic glow that tries and fails to conquer dusk. When dusk arrived, Vanning told himself to go out and get something to eat.

There was a lot of satisfaction in that, knowing he could still go out. That part of the situation was the best part, the fact that they didn't know where he lived. Or to put it another way, they didn't know where he was hiding out. It was sensible to look a thing like this in the face, because there was a great deal of difference between a home and a hiding place.

Chapter Eight

In the Fraser apartment the phone rang. She raced to it. And the first thing he said was a big thank you, thanks for everything.

"You feel better?" she said.

"I'm with him again."

"I knew that," she said. "I knew it the moment I heard your voice."

"I wanted to call earlier—"

"Of course—"

"But I couldn't get away. I've been with him ever since he came home this morning."

"You sound so excited."

"I ought to be," he said. "Something's happened. It's big. He's home now and I have a chance to breathe. I just checked with Headquarters. They told me he called Denver. The call was traced and they put two and two together. I knew he was making a long call but I couldn't do the tracing myself. Too many booths in the drugstore. A big place on Madison Avenue. He called Denver and pretended to be a newspaperman. He told them what they already knew.

79

Denver can't figure that one out. Neither can Headquarters. But I think I can."

"You mean he's working toward giving himself up?"

"Not yet. I figure he wanted to find out how much they knew."

"Wouldn't a smart criminal do that?"

"No," Fraser said. "A smart criminal would know for sure they'd trace the call. Everything he's done today backs up my ideas about the case. When he left the drugstore he got in a cab. I followed him. Somehow he knew he was being followed and he managed to lose me."

"How did you find him again?"

"He went back to his apartment. He's there now, across the street. I'm watching the front door."

"He got away from you and then he went home?"

"Right."

"He must be stupid."

"Not stupid," Fraser said. "It's just that he isn't operating like a guilty party. That phone call to Denver. And then knowing he was being followed. And coming back to his apartment instead of leaving town. A guilty man wouldn't do things like that."

She sighed into the phone. "I guess I'm thick. I just don't get it. You say he's a killer and yet he isn't guilty."

"I know. It sounds all mixed up."

"Why do you think he's staying in town?"

"I've got an idea he wants us to find those other men."

"Why?"

"I don't know," Fraser said. "I'm trying to hit an answer."

"What did Headquarters say?"

"They wanted me to bring him in. I begged for more time."

"How much more?"

"Not long," Fraser said. "Forty-eight hours."

"Do you have a plan?"

"Vaguely."

"Anything to work on?"

"Just Vanning. I better hang up now, I'm beginning to worry again. Vanning isn't enough. I need something else. It's like waiting for rain in the desert."

"Maybe you can talk to him again."

"If I could find a good excuse."

"But there's only forty-eight hours—"

"Don't remind me," he said. "Every time I look at my watch I get sick."

"Does it make you feel better, talking to me?"

"A lot."

"Stay there and talk to me."

"All right, dear."

"Tell me things."

"Things you don't know already?"

"Anything you want to tell me."

"Even if it's unimportant?"

"Even if it's silly," she said.

"Headquarters told me something funny," he said. "I shouldn't even mention it. I haven't any right to think about it. Not at this point, anyway. It all depends whether you're in a mercenary mood."

"I'm in any mood you're in."

"I don't know what mood I'm in, dear. I only know right now money's a side issue. Now I wish I hadn't said anything."

She laughed. "You've already opened your big mouth."

"How much do we have in the bank?"

"Seventeen hundred."

"Headquarters got a wire from Seattle," he said, and felt rather cheap saying it. But he was thinking of his wife and his children and the things he wanted to give them, and underneath that he was impelled by the desire to talk, to talk about anything except the big worry at hand, and he might as well talk about this; at least it was something practical, it was a basis for talk. And he said, "If I can get Vanning to tell where the money is, I'll get a reward of fifteen thousand."

"Fifteen thousand?"

"That's a lot of cabbage."

"Fifteen thousand."

"Let's both forget about it."

"We might as well. Even if you bring him in, he'll never own up."

"I'm sorry I mentioned it."

"Don't be sorry," she said.

"We'll forget about it."

"Sure."

"How are the kids?"

"Fine."

"And how are you?"

"Oh, I'm—"

"I've got to hang up," Fraser said. "He's out there, coming out of the house. Talk to you later—"

The receiver clicked. She lowered the phone. She started to light a cigarette, but suddenly there was a commotion in the next room and it sounded as though the children were beating each other over the head. She put down the cigarette and tightened her lips as she went in to break it up. As she entered the room the riot came to an immediate halt, and the three of them looked at her with innocent faces. She tried to appear severe, but she wasn't much good at this and all at once she laughed lightly and the children started to laugh and she ran at them, gathered them to her, hugged them and kissed them and said happily, "You little Indians—"

Chapter Nine

The restaurant was a popular seafood establishment, noted especially for its lobster. Vanning ordered a cup of clam broth and a large lobster. He ate slowly, getting pleasure from the rich pink-white meat dripping butter. It was luxury, this lobster. It was one of the things that made life worth living. There were considerable things that made life worth living. Luxurious things, rich, colorful things, tasty things, and then the quietly pleasant things, abstract things, certain contentments that couldn't be analyzed in terms of statistics. He thought of those things for a while, but only a little while. The lobster brought him back to the other things, and he found himself thinking in terms of the luxurious, the joys in a materialistic category. Somewhere along that path a few colors entered. There was deep rose against a background of rich tan. There was shining gold. There was blue, a good, definite blue, not bright, not at all watery, but deeply blue. And then the tan again. Healthy tan. And all that added up, and it became Martha.

The thought became action, and Vanning's hand shot back and away from the table, went sliding into his coat pocket. For a moment it wasn't there, and he told himself if it wasn't there it was no place. Then it came against his fingers, and he took it out of his pocket, the folded paper secure and actual and living against the flesh of his fingers. He unfolded it. He looked at the name. Just Martha. And then the address.

It was a fake address, of course. It had to be fake. If she was clever enough to fool him as she had done, she would certainly be clever enough to give him a fake address. He congratulated himself on the deduction. And yet that was all it amounted to right now. Nothing more than a deduction. In order to make it a fact he had to check on that address.

All right. Granted that the deduction was faulty and she actually lived there. He wouldn't be able to do anything about it. Certainly he had nothing to gain from it. Or maybe he did have something to gain. Maybe if he played fox sufficiently well, he could have his cake and eat it too. The folded paper with her address on it would give him a potential contact with John, without giving John a contact with John's quarry.

It was an important consideration. Potential contact with John. It was important on the surface, much more important beneath the surface, but he didn't feel like going into that now. There was something vital and glowing in the possibility that the address was on the level. It was an exceedingly vague possibility, but there it was, and Vanning told himself there would be a change of mood tonight. The hunted intended to do a little hunting.

He wasn't in too much of a hurry. He treated himself to a dessert of cherry cream pie. Then black coffee. Then a brandy and another brandy and a cigarette. Walking out of the restaurant, he felt well nourished and the taste in his mouth was a good taste, and even though it was starting out as another hot, sticky night, he felt cool inside. And calm. And strangely self-assured.

The address was on Barrow Street. To get there he had to

cross Christopher and Sheridan Square and that took him past the bar where he had met her. As he passed the bar, a feeling of boldness came over him, there was the desire to gamble. He turned around. He smiled.

He entered the bar, and almost instantly he recognized the fat beer drinker of the preceding night. The fat fellow was right there at the bar, and again he was drinking beer.

Vanning walked up, gestured to the bartender. As the man in white apron approached to take the order, the fat fellow turned and looked at Vanning.

"Well, now, what do you know?"

"Hello," Vanning said. He smiled at the bartender. "A brandy and water chaser for me. A beer for my friend."

The bartender nodded and went away.

"Another hot night," Vanning said.

"What brings you in here?"

"What brings anyone in here?"

"We're speaking about you. In particular."

"I'm looking for her," Vanning said.

"I knew it." This was said with tight-lipped emphasis. "I was willing to bet on it. One of those things that have to happen."

"As sure as that?"

"Like that," the fat fellow said, and he snapped his fingers.

"You make it seem like arithmetic."

"And that's what it is. Two and two makes four and you can't get away from it. Or maybe I should say one and one makes two. Now wait—" And the fat fellow frowned and ran a fat finger through a puddle of beer on the bar. "We have a problem here. Sometimes one and one doesn't make two at all. One and one makes one. You see what I'm getting at?"

"Nup."

"You'll see. Just follow me. I promise you, I won't go into a long production. I'll make it simple. Like this. You and that girl, you're a natural team."

"You do this often?"

"Do what?"

"Play Cupid."

"It's the first time. I usually look out for myself. But that deal last night, it was different, it was one of those sensational things. A setup if I ever saw one. I said to myself when I walked out of here, I said, I'll give ten to one he looks at her. Small odds, at that. and I said, I'll give five to one he gets to talking with her. Then the odds went up again. Twenty to one he likes her. Fifty to one she likes him. A hundred to one they walk out of here together."

"Keep it up. You're making money."

The fat fellow misinterpreted Vanning's mild sarcasm. The fat fellow said, "All right, even if it didn't happen last night, it's bound to happen. You and that girl are a combination. In every way. Mark my word, it's going to happen. Just as sure as I'm alive, I know it. And it makes me feel good. I don't know if I'm getting this idea across, but I feel terrific, just thinking about you and that girl. You in a full-dress suit, and the girl in white satin. Gorgeous, there's no other word for it. And I go past that, I get a picture of the two of you, I see you on a train together, I see you on a boat, on the boardwalk in Atlantic City or someplace. I keep on going. I get such a kick out of it. I get a picture of what your kids will look like. Chubby kids, all of them blond, all of them healthy, rosy faces just like her face, and blue eyes, and—"

"All right, that's all."

"What's wrong? What did I say?"

"Nothing. That's the point." Vanning sighed and shook his head slowly. "Don't get me wrong. I'm not sore. You're a nice guy. But I don't want to listen to you any more. I don't want to see you any more."

"Don't leave. I hardly ever get to talk to anybody. Let me buy you a drink. I promise to keep my big mouth shut."

"Sorry," Vanning said. "Thanks a lot, but you're such a good pal that you give me the blues."

He walked out. And it was all gone, that good feeling from the lobster and the brandy and the technical line of thought. It was replaced by a certain amount of confusion and some despair mixed in, and some loneliness and some bitterness, and topped with a dash of desperation.

The house on Barrow Street was a four-story white brick affair, externally in good shape. On a panel at right angles to the front door there was a list of the tenants, with a button adjoining each name. Vanning struck a match and looked for a Martha. He went down past a Mr. and Mrs. Kostowski, a Mr. Olivet, a Mrs. Hammersmith, a Miss Silverman, and then there was only one more name and it wouldn't be the name he wanted. It was absurd to think she had been fool enough to have given him a level address.

He looked at the name. He brought the match closer to the panel. And there it was, Martha Gardner.

A forefinger went thudding into the little black button. Then there was waiting. The finger hit the button again. more waiting. Then a buzzer, and Vanning opened the door and came into a small, neatly laid out foyer. Whoever took care of this place really believed in taking care of it. Vanning walked up a stairway carpeted in dark green broadloom. The walls were white, really white, blending with the quiet that flowed evenly through each straight and stolid hallway. There wasn't much light, just enough of it. She lived in a place where people obviously lived quiet lives.

As he came to the third floor, a door opened for him. Light from the hall hit the doorway, merged with bright light coming from the room, and flowed down and framed her face.

She was wearing a bathrobe, quilted blue satin. He expected her to step back into the room and close the door. And if she didn't do that, he expected her to stare, or gasp, or register some other form of surprise. She didn't do any of that. She even disregarded his damaged face. There was no particular response other than the ordinary process of standing there and looking at him.

"Remember?" he said. "You gave me your address."

"What do you want?"

"I would like to straighten things out."

"I don't think that's necessary."

"There's an explanation forthcoming."

"Really, I'm not interested in hearing your explanation."

Vanning frowned, taking that in and tossing it around for a few hollow moments. Then he offered her a dim smile and said, "You've got it backwards. What I meant was, there's explanation due from you."

This time she did the frowning. She looked at him and

yet she wasn't looking at him. She was looking at last night. He tried to gaze into her mind and gave it up after several crazy seconds.

Then she was saying, "All right, come in."

It was a small apartment, but it was clean, it was attractive, it went right along with the rest of the house. A living room with a studio couch, a bathroom and a kitchenette. Something about the colors and furnishings gave Vanning the idea that she had done her own decorating. The general scheme was blue and burnt orange, the blue demonstrating itself in various shades that climbed from the very pale to an almost black. A few passable water colors on the wall and one extremely interesting gouache.

He was looking at the gouache. He could hear her closing the door behind him. He told himself it was idiotic to have come here. There was a closet door not very far away, and he wasn't being at all absurd in juggling the possibility that John might be hiding in the closet. And yet he wasn't sorry he had come here, John or no John, he was here and he was satisfied to be here.

The gouache was simple and quiet and relaxed, showing a fishing boat in a lagoon, with sunset throwing dead blue and live orange onto the deck of the boat, the orange rising from the deck and flowing across green-gray water.

"Who did this painting?" Vanning asked.

"Pull yourself together. The name is on the bottom."

"Let's start over again. Where did you get the painting?"

"A little art shop on Third Street."

"It's an interesting job."

"I'm so glad you like it."

"Cut that out," he said, still looking at the gouache. "It doesn't go with the rest of you."

"Does that matter?"

"Yes," he said. He turned around and faced her. She had her arms folded, as if she were sitting in a jury box. "Yes, it matters more than you think. I want to know how you got tied up with those men. I want to know how a girl like you goes and lets herself wide open for a wrong play. You didn't belong in that picture last night and you know it as well as I do."

"Are you telling me I didn't belong?"

"I'm telling you."

"That's very funny," she said. "All day I've been telling myself I didn't belong in that picture."

"Why did you do it? Money? Sure. What else could it be? It had to be money."

"Do you always talk to yourself? Do you always answer your own questions?"

He didn't like what she was saying, and he didn't at all care for the way this was going, but he had to admire the way she was handling herself, the way her voice remained calm and level, the way she stood there, very straight, balanced nicely on her two feet without making too much of an effort at it.

"Why did you do it?" he said. "Why did you go to work for them?"

"I wasn't working for them. But suppose I was? Would it make any difference? You did something wrong and you were running away and you were bound to be caught. That's all I know. I don't feel like knowing any more."

"Say, what are you doing? Are you fencing with me?"

"I wouldn't attempt that. I'm not smart enough, Jim."

"What?"

"Jim."

"Thanks. It was nice of you to remember."

"I couldn't help remembering. Tell me, Jim. What did you do? How did you get yourself involved with the police?"

He stared at her. He studied her eyes as though they were rough diamonds and he was about to operate. And then he said, "You thought those men last night were police?"

"Weren't they?"

Vanning let out a laugh, drew it in a tight knot of sound that kept on tightening until it became a grinding gasp. "I think I get it now," he said. "You really thought they were police. That's why you took off so fast. And they knew you had them figured as police. They put you in the role of stool pigeon, and that made you go away faster. As long as you thought they were police, as long as you had me down as some criminal being taken in, your only move would be to clear out of it and stay out. It was clever on their part. It was stupid on my part not to see through the whole thing. And yet I'm glad it worked out like that."

"But all this doesn't tell me anything. It goes around in a circle."

"Nobody knows that better than I."

"Jim." She was coming toward him, came close enough to touch him and then stopped. "Who are they? What's going on?"

"Why should I tell you?"

"I can't answer that. You'll have to answer it for yourself."

He moved away from her, sat down on the studio couch. She came over and sat down beside him.

She said, "Can I fix you a drink!"

"No."

"Smoke?"

"No."

"Can I do anything?"

"You can sit there and listen."

She sat there and listened. He talked for almost a half-hour. When it was all over, when there was nothing more to say, they looked at each other, breathed in and out in unison. He started a smile, worked at it, got it going, and she helped him out with it. Then she stood up.

"Sit there," she said. "Let's see if we can cool off with some lemonade."

He watched her as she walked away, moving toward the kitchenette, a little alcove all by itself. From where he was sitting, he couldn't see her in the kitchenette. Now he began to get all sorts of thoughts, and the thoughts jabbed at one another, and he told himself it didn't make any difference now. No matter what the thoughts were made of, no matter what their sum, he couldn't do anything with it. That was all right. He was even a little glad. All he wanted to do was sit here and wait for Martha to come back.

She came back with a tray. A pitcher of lemonade, a bowl of ice. And glasses. Lemonade filled a glass, and she offered it to him.

"Drink this," she said.

"You make it sound as if I'm sick and you're taking care of me."

"Drink it."

For a while all they did was sip lemonade. Then Vanning

put down an empty glass and he looked at her and said, "Do you believe what I've told you?"

"Yes, Jim. Do you believe me when I say yes?"

He nodded.

She put her hand against the back of his head, patted him as if he were her little son. "Go home now. Go to your drawing board and finish that work you were telling me about. Get it all finished. Then go to sleep. And please treat me to dinner tomorrow night?"

"Seven."

"Where?"

"I'll meet you here. Good night, Martha."

He walked out without looking back at her. Going back to his room, he walked rapidly. He was in a hurry to get at the drawing board, in a very great hurry.

Chapter Ten

Fraser told himself it was a matter of selection. He stood outside the white dwelling and watched Vanning going away. He had placed a little more than twenty yards between himself and Vanning during the walk from the bar to here, and he had remained across the street as Vanning entered the place, and he'd been hoping a light would show in one of the front windows. When it failed to show, he wondered on the feasibility of going up and visiting the back rooms. Somehow it hadn't seemed like a good idea. He'd had the feeling it wouldn't give him anything solid.

And now he stood here and watched Vanning going away. He had the choice of following Vanning now or going up and trying the back rooms. He had his own system of questioning people so that they gave answers they didn't think were usable but which Fraser was able to use. He would probably get something from one of those back rooms and yet he still had the feeling it wouldn't be enough, wouldn't be what he wanted.

He decided to stay with Vanning. He lit a cigarette and followed his man to the place where his man lived. He saw his man entering the place, and then he crossed the street, went up to the room he had rented, seated himself behind the dark window, and waited.

And he saw the light arriving in Vanning's room. He saw Vanning moving around in a preparatory sort of way. The binoculars picked up the bright spots and the shadows, and Vanning's eyes were distinct, they were the eyes of a man in confusion, a confusion that had some strange happiness mixed in. Tonight there was something different in Vanning. The binoculars took it all in and clarified it, but it was clear only on the visual side, and not in the analysis. For some reason Vanning was hopeful and perhaps just a bit cheery, and Fraser began to use his imagination and kept it up until he disciplined himself, told himself imagination was no part of science. It was all right in art, but this wasn't an art. This was on the order of mathematics.

The binoculars saw Vanning seating himself at the drawing board. There were manipulations with a soft pencil. Vanning would never be a matisse. He was much too precise. He went at it more like an engineer. He used a T-square and a slide rule. He leaned close to the work and studied it carefully after each movement of the pencil.

It was interesting to watch him at his work. He had a cigarette going and the smoke of it shot a straight rigid column of blue past his head, the column quite permanent because once the cigarette was lit he left it in the ash tray and paid no attention to it. When it was burned out he lit another and treated it the same way.

The pencil work completed, Vanning commenced mixing gouache pigments. This took a long time. Fraser sat there with eyes burning into the binoculars, telling himself three hundred thousand dollars was a fortune. A man with three hundred thousand dollars didn't have to sit up all night with T-squares and gouache and shoulders bent over a board. It was something he had told himself many times, and this time it was in the nature of a conclusion.

And yet there was another consideration, and it was evolved from the way Vanning addressed himself to his work. The thorough, accurate method, the painstaking manner in which he mixed the paint, the slow, careful application of paint to rough paper. Again Fraser said it to himself. An engineer, he said, a patient calculator. Perhaps a fanatic for doing things in a precise way. Doing this sort of thing, anyway. And the possibility of his doing other things in the same way could not be completely disregarded.

Fraser sat there and watched. And the longer he sat there, the longer he watched, the more subjective he became. The more subjective he became, the more he began to doubt himself. There was so much he didn't know. About zoology, even though he had read many books. About crystallography, even though at one time he had taken a course at the museum. About judo, despite having been taught by one of the true experts. About Vanning, even though he'd been telling himself he knew Vanning.

And about psychology, and neurology and man's way of thinking, doing things, reacting. The books were all good books and represented a great deal of study and experimentation and summaries based on years of formularizing. But the field was still in its infancy. There was so much as yet unlearned, even by the top people. And the top people were Fraser's tutors, and Fraser told himself he was a novice. If he'd been someone else examining Fraser, he would have called Fraser a naturally humble man. But he was Fraser. And he was calling Fraser a fool for having considered Fraser a walking textbook on Vanning.

There was so much he didn't know about Vanning. There was so much a man didn't know about other men. Conversation was an overestimated thing. Such a large part of conversation was merely a curtain for what went on in the mind. So many madmen were walking around and fooling people. It wouldn't be ridiculous to ponder the possibility that Vanning was a victim of dementia praecox, extremely shrewd about hiding it, underneath the disease a good man, but dominated by the disease, a murderer and a terror. Ponder that, Fraser told himself.

And ponder the other roads. Because there were many roads. The road he had selected could be the wrong road. And it was as though he was in a car and he was going up that road, and the farther he traveled, the more he worried about its being the wrong road. But like any man behind a steering wheel, he tried to tell himself he was steering straight. Rationalizing, he knew he was rationalizing. But he couldn't do anything about that. All he could do was sit there and worry about it.

In the binoculars, Vanning labored with a paintbrush. The interior of the binoculars gradually became a magnetic little world. Fraser became a magnetized object being drawn into the little world. And as he arrived there, he talked to Vanning.

He said, "Tell me about yourself."

Vanning's lips did not move. He was concentrating on the drawing board. But somehow he said, "I'm a man in a lot of trouble."

"I know that," Fraser said. "Tell me about it."

"Why should I? Would you help me?"

"If I believed you deserved help."

"How can I make you believe?"

"Just tell me the truth," Fraser said.

"Sometimes truth is a very odd thing. Sometimes it's amazing and you refuse to believe it."

"The front of this thing is amazing. I'll understand if the background's the same way."

"I don't think you would," Vanning said. "I don't think any man would."

"Try me out."

"No," Vanning said. "I'm sorry but I can't take the chance."

"Don't you want to get out of this mess?"

"Getting out of it is very important to me. Staying alive is more important."

"Don't you trust me?"

"I'm in a position where I can't trust anyone."

"Is that all?" Fraser said.

"I'm afraid so. I'm sorry."

Fraser was about to ask another question, but just then the little world was blanketed with darkness. It became a black, meaningless thing until he took the binoculars away from his eyes and realized he'd been watching Vanning in the process of leaving the drawing board, getting into bed, switching off the light.

The room across the street was dark, a room of sleep, and Fraser liked the idea of getting some sleep himself. He liked the idea very much. He smiled wistfully at the idea, brought his chair closer to the window, leaned an elbow on the sill and sat there with his eyes half opened, waiting.

Chapter Eleven

There was a feeling that sleep would come easily tonight. When it finally reached Vanning it was like a vapor closing in on him. He rolled around in it, he floated down through it, down and down, going through the endless tides of thick slumber. And somewhere down there the tide twisted, started up in an arc, brought him toward the surface. He attempted to fight the tide, but it kept pulling him up in that circle. When it had him on the surface, when his eyes were wide open and he was staring at the black ceiling, he tried to continue the circle, go down again. But he couldn't close his eyes.

Worry was doing this. It couldn't be anything except worry. He was in her apartment again and he could hear himself talking to her he could hear the replies she was making. And dancing around somewhere in there was an unsatisfactory element, and he wondered what it was.

All at once he jumped out of bed and switched on the light. On a Governor Winthrop desk the alarm clock announced three-fifteen. He remembered leaving her apartment at nine-thirty or thereabouts. He measured it with his fingers. An intervening time of approximately six hours.

That was a long time. It was too long. It was time wasted, and he had to stop making these errors. Especially the kind of errors that concerned a woman. He had started out tonight on a mechanical basis and that was good, and he had allowed himself to fade from the mechanical to the emotional and that was very bad. She had given him nothing, anyway nothing that he could use. And he had given her plenty. He had given her everything. If she felt like using it, there was no limit to what she could do with it. And she could do a great deal in six hours.

He didn't bother to tie his shoelaces. He tripped once going down the stairway, saved himself from a complete fall by grabbing the rail. On the street he started out with a fast walk, ended up with what amounted to almost a sprint. And then he was panting as he stood outside the white brick house on Barrow Street.

The button was beside her name on the panel, and it was a shiny button and it was tempting. But he found himself thinking in terms of an alley. He walked around the side street at right angles to Barrow, and there was a narrow alley and the first thing he saw against the blackness of the alley was a light showing from a rear window on the third floor of a house facing Barrow.

Without counting the houses he knew it was that house.

Moving down the alley, he was figuring at first on a rear entrance, and wondering how he would get past the lock. And then he noticed a garden court, one of several garden courts at the other side of the alley, and the trees came into focus, and a few of them were quite high. One in particular was getting considerable play from the light that flowed out through the window. The light dipped and hopped through the upper branches of the tree, made puddles of silver on black leaves.

He walked up to the gate that separated the alley from the garden court. For a few moments he stood there, looking up at the shining leaves, rubbing his hands together, and then lightly, quickly, he climbed over the gate, he approached the tree. Again he looked up. Again he rubbed his hands together. Then he took off his coat.

It wasn't an easy climb. This was a very big tree, big in every way, particularly in the thickness of the trunk. In several places the trunk was much too smooth, and he felt himself slipping, felt the strain on his legs, told himself to stop being in such a hurry. He rested awhile, then went on climbing, took hold of a branch, pulled himself up, and now he was going up through the branches, the leaves swishing against his face.

A few thin branches gave him trouble, and he had to come in toward the center of the tree, where there was more thickness. Then up a couple more feet, and a couple more, and just a couple more. He turned slowly, to face the lighted window.

He saw her in there. She no longer wore the blue quilted

satin bathrobe. Now she was wearing a yellow dress trimmed with green. There was a cigarette in her mouth and she had a highball glass in her hand. She moved toward the window and turned so that her back was to the window. Then she moved again to the side, and he couldn't see her. There was only the lighted window and the motionless room beyond the window. And Vanning waited.

A shadow fell across the light. Vanning leaned forward. He saw her again. She was back at the window, and he saw her in profile. She was smiling. Her lips were moving. She took a drink from the highball glass. She took a puff at the cigarette. Vanning's fingers twisted, pressed into the branch that supported him. He saw her gesturing with the cigarette. Then once again she walked away from the window, out of sight.

There was another wait. It lasted a few years. Then the shadow again, falling across the light. And Martha again, leaning against the window sill. And then another shadow, falling across Martha, remaining there.

And then a hand, holding a highball glass. A man's hand, a man's coat sleeve. Cigarette smoke between Martha and that hand. And no motion now, nothing, only another wait. But suddenly a quick movement on the part of Martha. She was going away from the window. The other things remained there, the man's hand, the highball glass, the coat sleeve. And gradually the coat sleeve moved out across the lighted space, and there was a coat, and a shoulder, and a man's head, turning slowly and getting into profile. And there he was.

John.

Chapter Twelve

It was enough. It was hollow and yet there was a shattering in it. Vanning began his descent. He sighed a few times, he shook his head a few times, and as he came onto the ground he hit his fists together lightly, shook his head again, and then he grinned. He wasn't angry at John. He wasn't angry at anybody, not even himself.

He had to pass out a little credit. Some of it to John for engineering the thing from the beginning, but more of it to her, because her performance had been sheer perfection. Every move, every word, the smallest gesture, she had carried it out in major-league style. If this was the work she had cut out for herself, she was certainly doing it on a blue-ribbon basis.

As he walked down the alley, getting his arms through the sleeves of his coat, he knew he was rationalizing, but it didn't bother him. He was too tired to be bothered by anything right now. He was at the point where the open-field runner had already run past him and he had tried for the tackle and missed, and now all he could do was rest back on his elbows and listen to the crowd cheering the other team's touchdown.

He was going up the side street, turning, coming onto Barrow, and he was making his way along Barrow, listening to his own footsteps breaking through the quiet black. There seemed to be an echo to his footsteps. There seemed to be noise beyond the echo. Then the echo and the noise came together and moved up toward him, and he stopped dead and waited, and the sound now was purely that of footsteps behind him, and coming closer. And he waited there.

"That's right," a voice said. "Just wait there."

Vanning turned. He saw the man. It was quite dark around here, and yet he began to get the feeling he had seen this man before. And then he saw the gun.

"Will I need this?" the man said, and he pointed to the gun in his hand.

"You'd better keep it ready."

"I'll put it in my pocket," the man said. "Lift your arms a little. I want to see what's on you."

The man had the gun in his pocket as he came toward Vanning, and he hit Vanning lightly, swiftly, in the frisking process. Then he stepped back and waited for Vanning to do something.

"What do you want?" Vanning said.

"I'm not sure yet."

"Make up your mind. It's past my bedtime."

"Let's walk," the man said.

They walked down Barrow, crossed Sheridan Square. The man seemed to be walking at Vanning's side, but actually he was just a little to the rear.

"Let's walk to the park," the man said. "I want to have a talk with you."

"Why the gun?"

"Guess."

"Police?"

"You guessed it." And the man displayed a badge.

"I'm glad," Vanning said. "You don't know how glad I am. Now it's off my hands. Now it's your worry.

"My name is Fraser."

"Who cares what your name is? Who wants to know your story? You're the police and you're taking me in. Why don't we leave it at that?"

"Because there's more to it than that."

"All right, take me in and we'll find out."

"We're going over to the park and have a talk."

"You're the doctor."

"Now that's funny, your saying that. I always wanted to be a doctor. Maybe I am, in a way. I like to think it's possible for me to help people, rather than make their lives miserable. Lately I've been studying psychology."

"Good for you."

"I'd appreciate it if you helped me out."

"With your homework?"

"Call it that."

"Take me in, will you? just take me in."

"We're going to the park."

"I'm tired," Vanning said. "You don't have any idea how tired I am. I'm glad you finally grabbed me and I wish you'd take me in."

"Why did you do it?"

"Oh, come on," Vanning said. "Don't start that now. I'll get enough of that later."

"You must have had a reason. We never do things like that without a reason."

"Read tomorrow's late edition and you'll find out all about it."

After that the detective was quiet. They crossed another

street, went down another block. They were entering Washington Square Park. They went across grass, came onto pavement, and the detective gestured toward a bench.

They sat down. The detective took out a pack of cigarettes. "Have one?"

"Anything to make you happy," Vanning said. Then he smiled wearily. "No, I don't mean that. You're only doing your job. I'll have a cigarette, thanks."

The detective lit a match. Smoke sifted between the detective and Vanning.

They took in more smoke and blew it out and watched it rise. Then the detective said, "I've had my eye on you for quite a time."

"You don't need to tell me."

"You felt it?"

"No. You fooled me. But I'm not surprised. I should have known."

"Of course," the detective said. "The way you were running down that street. I could even see your shoelaces were untied."

Vanning frowned at the smoke. It made a weird pattern in front of his eyes. Some of it boomeranged and got into his eyes and he blinked. But he kept on frowning.

"All right," the detective said. "What's your name?"

"Van—"

"What?"

"Van."

"Van what?"

"Van Johnson."

"Be reasonable."

"Van Rayburn."

"That's an unusual first name. Van."

"Johnson does all right with it."

The detective made himself as comfortable as the park bench would allow. He took a long pull at the cigarette. "Now let's see," he said. "I'm walking down the street at three-thirty in the morning and I gander a man going someplace in a big hurry. Really flying. So I figure I'll stay behind and see what happens. So I follow this man as he tears down Barrow Street. I watch him go up the side street and the alley. I watch him climbing the tree. At first I figure too

99

many Tarzan pictures, but then I notice he's got himself across from a lighted window. So then I figure a Tom. I've still got to figure a Tom. That is, unless you can talk your way out of it."

Vanning looked at the detective.

"And that's all?"

"Why? Is there something else?"

"No," Vanning said.

"Tell me, Van. What's troubling you? Don't you have a girl friend?"

"I did," Vanning said. "At least I thought I did. Until a little while ago."

"That's the idea," the detective said. "Now tell me all about it."

"I was with her earlier tonight," Vanning said. "I accused her of playing around with another party. She said it wasn't true. So I took her word for it and went home. I couldn't sleep. I had to find out for myself. Without her knowing. That's why I climbed the tree and looked in the window."

"He was in there with her, wasn't he?"

"What do you think?"

"I don't think. I know. All I had to do was get a good look at your face. Tell me, Van, what do you do for a living?"

"Commercial artist."

"Okay," the detective said. He stood up. "That's all, Van. Go on home. Forget about her. If she lied to you once, she'll lie again. If you allow yourself to see her any more, you deserve every kick in the pants you get."

Vanning came up from the bench and faced the detective. "You're letting me go?"

"Why not? All you did was climb a tree."

Vanning turned and walked away. After a while he felt choked up and the pain in his lungs was a suffocating pain. He wondered why that was happening, then gradually realized it was because he was holding his breath. The stale air came out in a violent rush. He breathed in pure air. He breathed it in with desperation, as if he were in a tube where there was very little air remaining.

The streets paraded toward him like collections of black shapes, living but not moving. They instilled a definite discomfort, and he was in a hurry to arrive at his room. When he got there, he opened the door with a rapid, jerky motion, closed it the same way. Then he leaned back against the door and looked at the room.

"Well," he said, "we're still here."

He went into the bathroom, splashed cold water on his face. Doing it with his hands didn't give him as much cold wetness as he felt he needed. He put a stopper in the drain opening, filled the bowl with cold water, ducked his head in it, kept that up for several moments. When he lifted his head he saw himself in the mirror. He grinned at himself.

"All you did was climb a tree," he said.

The face in the mirror grinned back at him for a few seconds. Then, when it stopped grinning, it became expressionless.

"Buck up," Vanning said without sound. "It's not that bad. Give me the grin again."

The face stared back at him.

"What's the kick?" Vanning said. "Tonight you got a real break. You ought to be happy. You're a lucky boy tonight."

And without sound the face said, "Tonight was tonight. But then comes tomorrow."

"Get off the gloom wagon, will you? They say tomorrow never comes."

"They're all wet."

"You're all wet," Vanning said. "Dripping wet. You give me the blues, brother. Sometimes you make me sick. Why don't you go to sleep?"

"I'll try."

"Don't worry. You'll sleep."

"I hope so."

"Sure, you'll sleep. All you've got to do is close your eyes and think about nothing."

"It sounds easy, but sometimes the thoughts keep coming in like sticky air through an open window. You can't keep it out. The more you try, the faster it comes in. You have a date with her tomorrow night at seven o'clock. See how it is? There's your tomorrow. You'll think about that. You'll think about John. You'll think about Denver. What's that name again? Harrison, wasn't it? You killed Harrison. See if you can get away from that. You killed him, that's all there is to it, and they know you killed him, and now you're started, so you might just as well think about Seattle, and there's where the three hundred thousand comes in, so that brings you to the satchel. You're really moving now. You're wondering again, wondering as you've wondered a thousand times already, wondering why John left you in that room in the hotel, left you alone in there with the gun and the satchel, and somewhere in that there's an ounce of maybe, a fraction of an ounce. Maybe if you could figure that one out you'd have a door that you could open, you'd have something to give a lawyer, you'd have some actual ammunition on your side. Try to figure it out. Try to figure out the whole business. There must be an answer somewhere. You see the way it is? How can you keep these things out of your mind? Where did you drop that satchel? How can you fall asleep?"

"If I only had someone to talk to."

"Me."

"You? Don't make me laugh. You help me out like iodine helps sunburn."

Later, when his head came against the pillow, the pillow felt like granite. He tried to tolerate it, but after a while it was unbearable, and he sat up, switched on the bed lamp. He lit a cigarette.

In an ash tray near the bed, the stubs became a family that grew through the night.

Chapter Thirteen

For a man leading a normal life it would have been a pleasant day. The weather was pleasant, there was a bright sun, but an ocean breeze came up the Hudson and gave Manhattan a break. There was a good breakfast, and a smooth bus ride uptown. Fifth Avenue seemed lively and contented, perhaps just a bit smug, but then Fifth Avenue could afford that.

In the advertising agency, the art director was pleased with the work and handed out another assignment. That was nice. The deadline was generous, and that was even nicer. Lunch was nice too. And Fifty-seventh Street was showing some extremely interesting work by some new people, and so the remainder of the afternoon went riding along gently and at just the right speed.

In one of the larger galleries on Fifty-seventh Street he became engaged in a conversation with one of the more successful surrealist painters, and the two of them moved along from oil to oil, discussing the importance of shadow in surrealism, the effect of color on shadow, the effect of shadow on color, the effect of color and shadow on line, and it became one of those conversations that could very easily go on for years. The surrealist was more than a little interested in Vanning's point of view, and the whole thing led to a dinner invitation. Politely refusing, Vanning said he already had a dinner date for tonight.

"Oh, I'm sorry."

"So am I."

"Maybe you can break it."

"I could do that. But I don't think I will."

"Business?"

"In a way. Maybe some other time. All right?"

"By all means," the painter said. "I'll be here every day through the end of August, when the exhibition closes. You do like my work?"

"Very much. It has depth. It has technique. Very fine technique. You'll go places, I'm sure of it."

"It makes me so happy to hear that. I'm going to tell my wife about you. There's so much in what you say about painting. You don't talk like the ordinary experts. Your judgment is so fair, so objective, so calm. I don't usually tell my wife these opinions expressed toward my work. As a matter of fact, I only tell my wife the things that affect me deeply. You see, I have a very deep feeling toward my wife. We've been married for sixteen years."

Vanning stared at an open space of wall above the highest painting. "Why do you people pick on me?"

"I beg your pardon?"

Vanning kept staring at the wall. "Why do you rub it in?"

"I'm sorry. I fail to understand."

"Skip it. I didn't say anything. I do that every now and then. Don't mind me. Here, let's shake hands. I hope you and your wife will always be happy together. There's nothing like having a wife and being madly in love with her. Is there?"

On the painter's face a perplexed look gave way to a shining smile, and as he shook hands with Vanning he said, "My wife means everything to me. More than my art. That's why I'll never be a truly great painter. But it doesn't matter. Success in love is success in life. Are you married?"

Vanning nodded. He said, "It isn't a good marriage. I don't trust her. I ought to let her go. I know she's bad for me. That's the practical side. The other side of it is way over my head."

"Give her a chance. She's only a human being. And she's probably young. She can be molded. You listen to me. I'm much older than you. In the beginning, in Paris, my wife gave me a lot of trouble. She was a little imp. You know what I did once? I went on a hunger strike. After two days of that she got down on her knees, she cried like a little child. I told her I would eat if she prepared the kind of dinner I liked. She prepared a feast. We feasted together. We got drunk. We laughed ourselves unconscious. That's living, my friend. That's loving."

"You have something there."

"Fight with her. Make some noise. Give her excitement. Give her color. Give her children. My wife and I, we have three girls and a little boy. Every night I come home to a festival, a beauty pageant, a delightful comic opera right there in the little house where I live. There's so much yelling. It's wonderful."

"I'll bet it is," Vanning said. He smiled. He patted the painter's shoulder and walked out of the gallery. On the street, walking south on Lexington, he kept on smiling, and very slowly a frown arrived and he was smiling and frowning at the same time, and it showed he was a man in deep thought, somewhat amused at what he was thinking, somewhat puzzled. And when the smile faded and the frown stayed there, it showed he was a man who had made up his mind about something.

There was an hour to kill. He walked, he looked in some windows, he did more walking, he went into a haberdasher's and bought several shirts, a few ties, a few pairs of socks. He splurged on a brocaded robe. Splurging like that on himself gave him an idea, and a little later he was buying a five-pound box of candy and a large bottle of expensive perfume. Then he went home and showered and shaved, got himself into one of the new shirts, stood in front of a mirror, experimenting with the new tie.

At a few minutes to seven he walked down Barrow Street.

Again the door was open when he reached the third-floor landing. She was all ready. She was smiling.

She took a step toward him. "My, but you look nice."

"Here's a little something I picked up." He was extending the fancy packages.

"For me?" She took the packages and stared.

"I was going to try fur, but I didn't know what kind you liked."

She didn't get that. He decided to let it pass. They were going into the room. She opened the packages. The big box of candy brought a murmur of delight. The ornate bottle of perfume caused her to step back, her eyes wide. He was watching her as if she were under a microscope.

Gesturing toward the perfume, she said, "You shouldn't have done that."

"Why not?"

"That's very expensive."

"Don't you think I can afford it?"

Her eyes were on the perfume. "That's an awful lot of money."

He didn't say anything. He was lighting a cigarette. It was starting out the way he wanted it to start. The gifts leading to a mention of money, the money a potential path to the satchel. It was up to her to guide the way along the path. He waited, telling himself to step along with extreme caution. The type he was dealing with was the most dangerous and clever of them all. On the surface a soft-voiced innocence, an unembroidered sincerity. Beneath the surface a chess player who could do amazing things without board and chessmen.

"Really," she said, "you shouldn't have spent all that money."

"It wasn't so much, considering."

"Considering what?"

He studied the way she was looking at him. "Consider-ing," he said, "what I have."

"I didn't think you had a lot."

"It all depends on what you mean by a lot."

She laughed. "Maybe you haven't told me everything about yourself."

"For instance?"

"Maybe you're heir to a fortune."

"That's possible."

"Should I guess again?"

"Sure," Vanning said. "Give it a try."

They stood facing each other, and it was as if lengths of foils separated them. He was trying to get rid of his own thoughts, his own strategy, trying to bring her thoughts into his mind so he could take a close look and figure how far she was ahead of him. Because even in this short time she had taken the lead, she was out there in front, her pace steady and yet relaxed, her confidence a thing of menace, her relaxed superiority almost like a panther's playing with a zebra.

"Maybe," she said, "you've been fooling me all the time and it's some sort of a gag. Actually you're a young wizard of Wall Street."

"Try again."

"You made a fortune playing cards."

"Do I seem as if I'd be clever at poker?"

"That's why you'd be clever. Because you don't seem to be clever. Or perhaps shrewd would be a better word. The shrewdest people give you the impression that they're exactly opposite."

"That's a keen observation," Vanning said. "I'm going to make a note of it and keep it on file."

"Do that. You'll find out it comes in very handy now and then."

"You still have another guess coming."

"Feed me first," Martha said. "I can think better on a full stomach."

They went out and found a restaurant. It was one of those places where people concentrated on food, and yet each booth was a little rendezvous in itself. There was an emphasis on privacy and yet it was a casual sort of privacy.

While they waited for their order, their conversation was affected by the atmosphere of the place and it became pleasant, meaningless chatter with a laugh here and there. She had a fine sense of humor, deviating in a marvelous way between the dry and the robust. For detached moments Vanning was enjoying her presence, and the worry and peril were completely out of it. She began telling him of amusing incidents at the glassware counter, and her imitations of various customers were definitely blue-ribbon. At one point his laughter came out in a burst, at another point he smiled and nodded appreciatively as she pantomimed to perfection the undecided buyer of glass.

When the steaks arrived, they stopped fooling around. It was phenomenal food and they gave it their undivided attention.

Later, while they sipped brandy, they looked at each other.

And Vanning said, "You still have that one more guess."

"Oh, yes. I forgot about that."

"I didn't."

"Are you trying to find out how smart I am?"

"I already know how smart you are," Vanning said. "Now I want to see how good you are at guessing."

"Suppose it isn't a guess?"

"If it isn't a guess it's deduction. If it isn't deduction it's mind reading and I'll put you in business on Broadway. Now let's have it. This is the big one."

He grinned at her. She didn't return the grin. A strange quiet became a bubble growing larger in the center of the table, and he could see her through the bubble. He could see her face, and that was as far as he could see. It frightened him, and he didn't know why. There was no reason for fright. The situation held no immediate danger. But he was very frightened, and gradually, as he sat there watching Martha, he realized that it was not Martha he feared. And it was not John. And it was not the police. It was himself.

And then all at once there was a bursting in his brain, and this place, and Martha, the table, the brandy, everything, it all assumed the substance and dimensions of a horrible reality. Horrible only because it was real, so very real that it refused to be reined in. He was in love with her.

It was not logical, it was impossible. And yet there it was. The attraction, the feeling were beyond measurement, beyond the limits of self-analysis. The thing itself was clear and definite, and yet the reasons were vague and far away and he had no desire to itemize those reasons. There was an eerie resemblance between this matter and something else that had happened to him, but right now he couldn't remember what that something else was. His mind was too busy accepting the fact, the ghastly truth that he had fallen in love with this woman. Shackles of some fierce, unbreakable metal were already locked, holding him secure. And that, too, was an awful paradox, because he had not the slightest wish to free himself. No matter what she was, no matter what she had done or was doing now, no matter what trouble and heartache the hidden Martha represented for him, he was in love with the Martha that showed herself to him now.

It was a phenomenon of huge proportions. It was bigger than life. And yet, as big as it was, there was something even bigger. And he knew what that was, too, only with this new realization there was no explosion, the knowledge reached him in a calm sort of way. He was certain she had fallen in love with him.

"I'm ready," he said.

"I'm thinking."

"Make it good."

"If it's too good," she said, "it won't be any good at all. It will wreck everything."

"I'm willing to gamble."

"Maybe that's because you don't have too much to lose."

"And you?"

"I'll be losing a lot. You have no idea how much I'll be losing. Do you mind if I back out?"

"Yes," he said. "I do mind. I want you to make that guess."

"It's not a guess any more. I'm sure I know. If I'm correct, the whole thing blows up in my face. If I'm wrong, you'll walk out on me and nobody can blame you. I don't want to lose you, Jim. Maybe you know that already."

"I've been playing with the idea."

"No matter what you are," she said, "I don't want to lose you."

He stared at her. She had repeated what he had told himself. And it was no act. Because she meant it, actually meant it, her eyes and her words were far more dreadful than an act, and he could think of only one explanation. There were two sides to Martha Gardner, and what he had thought was the hidden side was not hidden at all, it was actual, it was living breathing, performing. And doubtless she feared and hated that side of herself just as he did.

"You're halfway across the tightrope," he said. "You can't turn back."

"You're really asking for it, aren't you?"

"Put it another way. Say I'm demanding it."

A tinge of indignation came into her eyes. "You sound as if I'm obligated."

"We're both obligated. It's just about time to take off our masks."

"I don't know what you mean."

"I mean take off the masks. Walk off the stage. Remove the greasepaint. Any way you want to put it."

"I'm sorry, Jim." A confused little smile crept back and forth across her parted lips. "You have me in the dark."

"Do I really?" He leaned toward her, his eyes a set of lances.

She touched finger tips to her chin. "It's so strange, the way you're looking at me."

"I'm looking at the life ahead of me. With you."

She gave him a sideways glance. "I'm not bothering you, am I?"

"You don't catch the drift," he said. He bit a thumbnail. "Let's get out of here."

He paid the check. They left the restaurant. The Village was under twilight, and nothing much was happening on the street. They went down the street and came onto Fifth Avenue, and then they turned toward the arch that officially welcomed people to Washington Square. He was waiting for her to say something, knew she was waiting for him. Eventually he realized it was up to him.

"I'll let you in on something," he said. "I've been playing a game with you."

"You didn't have to tell me that." There was an ache in her voice.

"I thought it might do the trick. Crazy notion, wasn't it? Like trying to hook a marlin with trout bait. I never under-estimated your brains. It was just that I overestimated my own. Now I don't feel like fighting any more. Whatever it is you're trying to win, you've won it."

She stopped. She looked at him. And then all at once it came out and there was fury in it, pain in it as she said, "Don't throw puzzles at me. Don't try to twist me around and have fun with me. You told me a story and I believed you. Because I wanted to believe you. That's all it was. It was very simple. But you weren't satisfied with that. You had to make it complicated, with question marks in it, with me on one side of the fence and you on the other. I wanted to come over on your side, but you wouldn't have it that way. And I suppose I can't very well blame you. Who am I? Why should you share all that money with me?"

"Is that the guess I've been waiting for?"

"It's no longer a guess. I know. How could you expect me to know otherwise? Why would you keep digging away, trying to find out if I had suspicions?"

"You make it sound as though I'm a guilty party."

"Aren't you?"

"All right, let's assume I am. Let's assume I never lost that satchel, and now I have the three hundred thousand hid-den away in a nice safe place. What are you going to do about it?"

"Nothing."

"Oh, come, come. I'm a crook. I'm a killer. You don't intend going to the police?"

"I intend going home," she said. "I want you to leave me alone. From now on, I mean. Please—I don't want to see you any more."

"What you really mean is, this Martha doesn't want to see me any more. What about the other Martha? The other Martha, the bad one, the one who's up with John."

She gasped. Her eyes bulged and she stepped back, kept going back, suddenly pivoted and started to run. And it was as if goblins were chasing her. Vanning stood there, watching her as she ran away. When she was out of sight, he turned and went onto Fifth Avenue and got into a bus. He had no idea of where he wanted to go. The bus made its run, made a turn and got started with another run. At the end of the run Vanning got off and walked into a bar and stayed there for an hour, and then he walked across the Village and arrived at the place where he lived. He didn't feel like going to sleep. He wasn't at all tired. And it was still an early hour. He leaned against the iron rail of the front steps and put a cigarette in his mouth, looked across the street, took out a book of matches and started to light the cigarette, then dropped the lighted match and stared across the street. And the cigarette fell out of his mouth.

And the man came walking toward him.

Vanning just waited.

Chapter Fourteen

"Remember me?"

"What do you want?" Vanning said.

"I'll bet you don't even remember my name. I did give you my name, you know."

"I don't remember."

"Fraser."

"Oh, yes," Vanning said mechanically. "That's right."

"And you're Van."

"Van Rayburn."

"No," Fraser said. "That was last night when you climbed a tree and I had a father-and-son talk with you. Tonight you're Vanning. You're James Vanning."

"You have a nice change of pace."

"No, it's the same old routine day after day. I get pretty tired of it now and then, but I know what it's all about."

"I wouldn't bet against that," Vanning said. He took a deep breath. "I'm ready to go along with you now."

"I'm not ready yet," Fraser said.

"What do you want from me?"

"Why can't we stand here and talk?"

"That was last night," Vanning said. "Remember? The psychology attraction was last night. You've done your

111

jockeying already. Now you're in there for the kill. You've made it. You've done a wonderful job and now it's all over and what are we hanging around for?"

"If you don't mind, I'll handle it the way I think best. It's my case."

"I thought Denver had it."

"Denver gave it to New York, and New York gave it to me. I mean entirely. If anything goes wrong, it's all my fault. I'll get it from all sides. From New York and from Denver. And Seattle."

"I don't get Seattle."

"I told you they gave me the entire case. By that I mean the entire case. What I'm supposed to do now is take you in, then I look for the other two men."

"The other three men."

"See what I mean?" Fraser said. "You've already given me something."

"That's fine. What can you give me?"

"Every possible break. I don't think you're a killer."

"But I am."

"Why?"

"Self-defense."

Fraser put his hands in his coat pockets, thumbs overlapping the pockets. "Suppose we go up to your room and talk it over?"

He didn't wait for Vanning's reply. He walked past Vanning. He led the way up the stairs. It would have been easy for Vanning to take him from behind.

They both knew it. They didn't need to talk about it. Going up to the room, they remained quiet, as though they had something definite and logical ahead of them, as though they were members of a closely knit organization.

At the door, Fraser stepped aside. Vanning moved in, put his key in the lock, opened the door. Just before he walked in, he looked at Fraser's thin, sharp face. The sharp, black eyes. The black mustache. Fraser smiled at him. He responded with a wide grin, standing relaxed but very straight nevertheless, and he was breathing easily. It was as if a tremendous weight had been lifted from his shoulders.

Fraser walked over to the drawing board, stood there looking at it.

"Here's something else," he said. "You gave me some truth last night. You told me you were a commercial artist."

"I didn't tell you everything last night, but what I told you was true."

"You have anything to drink?"

"I'll make something."

"Plenty of ice. It's a scorching night."

Vanning prepared drinks, brought them in. There was some serious concentrating on the drinks, and then Fraser lowered his glass and said, "All right, I'm ready to listen. I want everything. Every move, every detail. I want the whole business, from the very beginning."

It lasted the better part of an hour. Fraser made only a few interruptions, and did that only when it was necessary to straighten out a sequence here and there. Vanning was speaking in a low voice, but without a stumble, without a repetition of facts. He was finding it easy to speak. Despite the low pitch, his voice was clear. Toward the end there was more than a little confidence in it.

When it was finished, Fraser walked toward the drawing board, tapped his fingers against it, turned and faced the chair where Vanning had one leg crossed over the other.

"Only one thing," Fraser said. "Only one thing bothers me. Let's go back to it. Let's put you back again in that hotel room in Denver. I'll see if I can repeat it the way you told me. You're in that room with John and Pete. They put you in the bathroom. They don't lock the bathroom door. They have a conversation in whispers. That's reasonable. Okay, you're waiting in the bathroom. Suddenly you realize there's complete quiet in that other room. You can't make that out. So finally you decide to take a chance. You open the door. And the other room is empty. But there on the bed you see a gun. And there on the dresser you see the satchel. And that, my boy, is a very strange state of affairs."

"If I could explain it, I would."

"That's understood," Fraser said. "At least I understand. But other people wouldn't buy it. In a courtroom they'd laugh at you. You see the spot we're in. That setup with the gun and the satchel. It doesn't add. It's fantastic."

"Then I guess I'm finished."

"Don't talk like that," Fraser said. "I'm an optimistic sort

113

of person, but if you lose your grip you'll only make it hard for me."

"I'll hold on."

"You've got to. We're going to work this out together. I'm convinced you're an innocent man, and I'll do everything in my power to bring you out of this. What we've got to do now is find the answer to that crazy picture in the hotel room. I don't think we'll find the answer here. What do you think?"

And he was looking at Vanning. It wasn't necessary to say anything. The look was a request, and Vanning took it in and examined it and knew what it meant. He thought of Martha. He thought of Martha's eyes. And her lips. And the way she walked. The sound of her. The presence of her. He told himself to put her out of his mind.

Fraser folded his arms, bent his head to the side, kept on throwing the look. Seconds built themselves into a full minute. And then Fraser said, "Well, what about it? Can you put us on the starting line?"

"I think so."

"Good. Far from here?"

"Barrow Street."

"I thought so. I had the house spotted, but there's more than one in that house."

They went out of the room. Walking down the street, they weren't going fast, they weren't going slowly. They walked side by side, two men going somewhere.

As they came onto Barrow Street, a shiver ran through Vanning, and after that he let out a sigh. Fraser was looking at him.

"What's wrong?" Fraser said.

"The girl."

"What about her?"

Vanning closed his eyes, pressed finger tips into his forehead. "I thought I had common sense," he said. "I thought I knew something about life."

They were standing still. Fraser was lighting a cigarette. "We all think we know something about life. We think we know ourselves. If we did know, we'd be adding machines instead of human beings. You're in love with that girl and you don't want to destroy her. You're very much in love,

114

because Vanning doesn't matter now, does he?"

"I can't get a practical thought in my head."

"Take a drag at this cigarette."

"That won't help. Maybe if you clipped me in the teeth—"

"That won't help, either. Let's see if we can take it from a long-range point of view. You think she was in on that Seattle affair?"

"I don't know."

"What about Denver?"

"I don't know."

"We'll make it dark. We'll make it as miserable as we can. Let's assume they had her working for them from the very beginning. Remember, we're stretching the point. All right, she helped out with the Seattle robbery. Probably a few jobs before that. And probably she has a prison record. Let's say she gets ten years. How old are you?"

"Thirty-three."

"You're forty-three when she gets out. Are you willing to wait?"

Vanning turned away from Fraser and stared down the street, his eyes soldered to the white brick front of the house where she lived. "I can't let it happen," he said. "I don't know what got her into this kind of life. I know she isn't made for it. She's such a healthy girl, she's full of living. She needs a guy. She needs a home. And kids. If they put her in prison, she'll decay. I want to see her laughing. I want to see her bending over a stove. Wheeling a baby carriage down the street. I can't see her behind bars. I can't see that."

Looking at his wrist watch, Fraser said, "If we get a move on, maybe we can put a head on this thing before morning."

"Ten years."

"Remember, I said it was the dark side."

"Promise me you'll do something for her."

"I'll be level with you. I can't promise anything. Once I bring her in, it's out of my hands."

"She wasn't in that station wagon. Maybe she had nothing to do with Seattle."

"Maybe."

"Everything is maybe. Everything."

"It's maybe as long as we stand here," Fraser said. "Why don't we go ahead and find out?"

"Do you need me there?"

"You'll have to face her sooner or later."

Vanning began to walk ahead. Fraser came up at his side. They were going down Barrow Street.

"Look what I'm doing," Vanning said. "Look what I'm doing to her."

"Think of what you're doing for yourself."

"I had to travel to Chicago by way of Colorado. I couldn't take another road. No, I had to go and use that road."

"And then you would have never met her in the first place."

"That's what I mean."

"So all right then," Fraser said. "It adds up to the same thing."

"No, it doesn't. I can't look at it that way. I guess I would have met her somewhere. I don't know. I was bound to meet her."

"Brother, you need a shot in the arm. You need a cold shower. You're in a bad way, do you know that? And if you go on like this, you won't be of much help to me. That means I won't be able to help you."

"Can't you help her? Can't you do something?"

"Not if she's a criminal. If she's a criminal, we've got to put her in prison. That's why society hires us. You'd be amazed how some of us hate our jobs. But somebody has to do this kind of work. Otherwise you'd see broken store windows and dead people all over the street. Now try to think along these lines." He turned and got a glimpse of Vanning's face. "No," he said, "don't even try. Don't think of anything. Just take me to that address."

They walked on. The houses marched past them in funereal parade. The house of white brick came nearer. The white stood out against the black street like something dead surrounded by mourners.

"That one," Vanning said. And he pointed.

"Come on."

They came to the door and Fraser looked at the panel bearing the tenants' names. "Which one is it?"

"Gardner."

Fraser pressed the button.

"Maybe she isn't there," Vanning said.

"We'll find out."

"Maybe she packed up and left."

"It's very possible."

"I guess that's what she did. She packed up and left."

"Sure," Vanning said. "That's what she did. If she was there, we'd get a buzz."

"I'll try again."

"There's no use trying. She's gone."

Fraser showed a pair of tightened lips. "And if she's gone," he said "your goose is cooked. Do you realize that? You can't take me to that house outside of Brooklyn. You told me you have no idea where it's located. If the girl is gone, we've lost our only contact. Think that over."

"I've thought it over already. I don't even care."

Again Fraser pressed the button; he held his finger against it as he watched Vanning.

And then there was a buzz, and Fraser said, "She's home."

"I didn't hear anything."

"I said she's home. We're going up." Fraser's hand moved down and touched a bulge in his coat pocket. "Come on, Vanning. This is the wind-up."

Fraser opened the door. He flattened himself against the door.

"You first," he said.

"Don't you trust me?"

"Not in the condition you are now. Do me a favor, will you? Don't make me use the gun. Please."

Vanning moved past Fraser, started up the steps, heard Fraser's footsteps behind him. The stairs and the walls seemed to have a high polish, seemed to glow in a way that made them unreal. The glow increased. Vanning told himself it was really that, it was unreal. When he came to the second-floor landing, he stopped.

Behind him, Fraser murmured, "Where is it?"

"Third floor."

"Up we go."

"This is hell."

"Climb."

They went up to the third floor, and her door was open and she was standing there and again she was wearing the quilted blue satin robe. When she saw Vanning, her eyes lit up. When she saw Fraser, her eyes widened and she stepped back into the room, leaving the door open, going back and back into the room, looking at Vanning, at Fraser, at Vanning again.

Fraser closed the door. He walked across the room as if he had lived in it for years. He pulled down the shade and turned his back to the window. He leaned against the window sill and folded his arms as he looked at Martha.

He said, "Sit down. I want to talk to you."

She moved toward a chair, her eyes on Vanning. She sat down and her eyes kept watching Vanning.

Fraser said, "Are you Martha Gardner?"

"That's my name."

Gesturing toward Vanning, the detective said, "Do you know that man?"

"Yes."

"Who is he?"

"James Vanning." Now, for the first time since the door had been closed, she took her eyes away from Vanning and faced the detective.

"We're going to step on the gas," Fraser said. "We're going to use a good, sharp knife and cut away everything that doesn't matter. Now, Miss Gardner, what do you do for a living? Fast. I want it fast."

"I sell glassware in a department store."

"How long have you worked there? No, we'll change that. How long have you been in New York?"

"Three years."

"And this address?"

"Five months."

"When you took that trip to Seattle, you went by train, didn't you?"

"I've never been to Seattle."

"All right then, in what town did you meet John?"

"John who?"

"Just John. Come on, Miss Gardner, come on."

She looked at Vanning. Suddenly she smiled at him. She

said, "What's the matter, Jimmy boy? Why do you look so sad?"

Vanning's gaze dropped to the floor. He was standing on his own two feet, and yet his whole body seemed to be dropping to the floor, going through the floor.

"We're talking about John," the detective said. "The man who was here last night. In what town did you meet him? When did you meet him?"

"Last night," she said. "In this room. For the first time."

"Really?"

"Really," she said. "I'll tell you about it, if you want."

"By all means. And you'd better make it good, Miss Gardener, because you're in a terrible jam."

"I don't think so," she said. "I'm not worried about it at all. I know everything is going to be all right." She turned and smiled at Vanning. "Isn't it, Jimmy?" And then she came back to Fraser and the smile went away and she said, "The man you call John, the man who was here last night, he told me his name was Sidney. He said he was an old friend of James Vanning. I'm quoting him now. Just as he said it. He said he had forgotten Vanning's address. He asked me if I knew. I told him I didn't know."

"How did he pick up your address?"

"I asked him that. He said Vanning had told him about me, and one day when they were walking down Barrow Street, Vanning pointed out the house where I lived."

"Did you believe him?"

"No."

"All right then, how did he find out your address?"

"I haven't the slightest idea."

"Then you're not connected with him?"

"No."

"Have you ever been in prison?"

"No."

"Now this John, or Sidney, or whatever his name is, what else did he tell you last night?"

"That was all. He just wanted Vanning's address. But he stayed for quite a while, trying to get it. He went at it in a roundabout way. I let him talk. I made him feel at home. I even gave him a few drinks. I didn't want him to catch on."

"What do you mean, catch on?"

119

"I know who he is."

"You don't have to keep your face so straight, Miss Gardner. You're not playing poker. You say you know who he is. How do you know?"

"Jimmy told me. Jimmy told me everything."

Fraser made a chin gesture toward Vanning. "Why do you call him Jimmy?"

"Because he's Jimmy."

Fraser took a pack of cigarettes from his coat pocket. He tossed the pack from one hand to the other. He said, "I think we're going around in a circle. We still don't have anything." His head went down, snapped up, his eyes jabbed at Martha and he said, "Are you really in love with that guy standing there?"

"Madly."

"You realize what a spot he's in?"

"Yes."

"And what a spot you're in?"

"Yes."

"Tell me, Miss Gardner, love is an important issue with you?"

"It's everything."

"Then why the devil don't you come clean?"

"I've told you all I know. I'll do anything you want me to do."

Fraser stood up. He walked across the room, reached the door, took a swing at it and pulled the punch. Then he started to turn, and then he stopped and his arms fell and hung loosely at his sides. And he just stood there.

That went on for several foolish seconds, but when the foolishness faded it faded quickly, energetically, and Fraser whirled, faced the door, went through rapid motions that got the door open and got the revolver out of his pocket, his finger against the trigger. And he stepped back into the room, beckoned with his other hand.

"Come on in," he said. "Open house tonight."

Chapter Fifteen

John came walking into the room. John was very surprised. He had a gun in his hand, but it wasn't pointing at anything in particular.

"Put the gun on the floor," Fraser said. "Don't start anything because then we'd both get hurt. Close the door, Vanning."

Vanning moved in behind John and closed the door. He stayed there, behind John, waiting.

Fraser took a step toward John and said, "I told you to put your gun on the floor."

"That's asking a lot," John said.

"I'm in a position to ask a lot."

Now John had lifted his gun and the two guns were pointed and ready, and John said, "I'm in a position to refuse."

"We can stay this way all night."

"I guess we can."

"Or else we can start shooting and get it over with."

"You play it your way and I'll play it mine."

Fraser bit his lower lip. He studied his own gun for a few moments and then, when his eyes lifted, his gaze rested on Vanning for a very small part of a second, and after that he was grinning at John and he was saying, "I'm not very good at this. My nerves can't take it."

He shrugged and tossed the gun away and watched it land on the studio couch. Just as the gun made contact with the upholstery, Vanning moved in and took hold of John's arm and did some twisting. John let out a moan and went to his knees. John's arm was far up behind his back and his limp fingers allowed the revolver to break loose. Vanning caught it before it could hit the floor. He walked away from John and gave the gun to Fraser. And Fraser put the gun in his pocket, stepped over to the studio couch and regained his own gun. He smiled at Vanning. He said, "That wasn't bad."

John was sitting on the floor and rubbing his arm. When

he started to get up, Fraser motioned him down with the gun.

"Just stay there," Fraser said. "We don't need to be formal about this."

"I'm a fool," John said. "And I guess guns don't like me. I've never had much luck with guns."

Fraser looked at Martha. And then he looked at John. His gaze went back to Martha, but he was addressing John as he said, "What about her?"

"She's not in it," John said.

"That's not enough. You'll have to tell me why. And it's got to be very good."

"Vanning can tell you why," John said. "We had him unconscious the other night, and while he was out I looked through his pockets. I wanted to see if I could find out where he lived. It was no go, he wasn't carrying any personal papers, not even a card in his wallet. Only a note with the girl's name and address on it. I copied the information and put the note back in his pocket."

Fraser looked at Vanning. "All right?"

Vanning wore a tired smile. He nodded slowly. He said, "It figures."

"Now then," Fraser said, putting himself in a chair, his eyes arrows, with John the motionless target, "you're in a position to make life miserable for Vanning. You understand that?"

"I can see it."

Fraser's eyes were almost closed, and it was as if his eyes were the fine lenses of a fine camera. He said, "It goes along this way, John. You're not exactly a young man any more, and if I'm guessing right, this manipulation is going to send you up for a long, long time. You won't be very happy in prison, but if you have any good in you, I think you'll sleep better at night knowing that you went to bat for our friend here."

John went through a brief facial contortion. He said, "I'm not comfortable here on the floor."

"Make yourself comfortable."

John stood up and walked to the nearest chair. He sat on the edge, his hands folded between his legs. There was a quiet, and it churned, and John stared at the wall across from him, and then there was a strange little interval during which John's eyes skipped from Fraser to Vanning to Martha and back to Fraser again.

It all came to a head. It broke, and John said, "Can we make an exchange?"

"We can trade facts," Fraser said. "Nothing else."

"That's what I want. The facts. I want to see where I stand. Let's hear what you have on your side."

"The main thing on my side is Seattle. I know you headlined the bank job. Three hundred thousand dollars. It points at you for so many reasons that we won't even bother to count them. Do you want me to keep talking?"

"I guess you've told me enough," John said. "It's a fair exchange. I only wanted to be sure about Seattle. That puts me in the soup, and there's no good reason why Vanning should be in there with me. He's clear."

"You'll stick with that?"

"He's clear," John said. "He had nothing to do with Seattle. He's an innocent man, but if you want that three hundred grand, only Vanning can tell you where it is."

"We'll come to that," Fraser said, and he looked at Vanning.

There was a moment of shock, followed by a moment of complete realization, and after that the first thing Vanning felt was a greatly multiplied admiration for Fraser's thinking power. That lasted for a few hazy moments, and it contained the knowledge that Fraser had taken him for a beautiful ride. But he couldn't hate the detective. He couldn't blame the detective. He couldn't blame anyone for doubting that story of the lost satchel. He was close to doubting it himself. In a frantic effort to erase the doubt, he hurled his mind back to Colorado, and he tried to see Denver, and a dark street in Denver became part of the swishing, droning circle that went round and round with no indication of a halt.

Fraser was lighting a cigarette. He went about it slowly, methodically. When he lifted his head, his eyes rested on John. "Let's have a look at Denver," he said. "If you really want to set things right for Vanning, you'll explain that business in the hotel. You'll explain why you left Vanning alone with the gun and the satchel."

"You ought to be able to figure that out. You're a detective."

"I'm not psychic."

John placed folded hands against the back of his head. "The whole thing was set up by Harrison. It was all his idea. I've never gone in for killing. I don't believe in it. I was trying to figure out a way to get rid of Vanning without killing him. I couldn't get any ideas, and finally Harrison convinced me that there was only one thing to do and the sooner we did it the better. Harrison said it was his job. He was a specialist at that sort of thing. He did it in terms of arithmetic. He always used to tell me there was no sense in risking a charge of first-degree murder when you could angle it toward second-degree or even manslaughter."

"You're taking me in deep," Fraser said. "Go a little deeper."

"Harrison was waiting there in Denver. So here's the way things stood. The bathroom door was unlocked. Vanning was in there and I was in the bedroom with another man."

"His name?"

"When you catch him," John said, "he'll tell you his name." He waited for that to sink in. Fraser nodded to signify that it had sunk in. And then John said, "Harrison knew the hotel we would use. He took a look at the register after giving us a high sign in the lobby. Then he came up to the room and the three of us talked it over. Harrison told us to go out and he would handle the rest of it. He said he wasn't taking any chances on a charge of first-degree murder. He said he was going to give Vanning a chance to put fingerprints on that gun. And if Vanning wanted to, Vanning could pocket the gun. Figuring on a percentage basis, Vanning would do that. He would pick up the gun and then he would put it in his pocket. Later on, if things developed the wrong way, Harrison could claim that Vanning made a try for him with the gun. No sense doing it in the hotel. Harrison wanted a dark street. A fast powder."

"Wasn't that doing it the hard way?" Fraser said.

"Harrison was very sure of himself. He was too sure of himself. That was a bad habit he had."

"Didn't you have any say?"

"I told him he was taking a big chance," John said. "But it was his play and I let him go ahead. He was sure it would work out. So what he did was to leave the gun on the bed and the satchel on the dresser, then go out and wait in the hall. And then out comes Vanning with the satchel and the gun, and what happens after that I've never been able to figure. What I mean is, the way Vanning came out on top, because Harrison was a very talented agent when it came to guns."

"I had the gun in my pocket." Vanning said it as if he was talking to himself. As if he was in the woods again running through the dark, trying to get away from the narrow street where Harrison's body grew cold.

"Sure you had it in your pocket," John said. "And that's why it's so mixed up. Harrison had a gun in his hand, didn't he?"

"Yes. He had the gun pointed at me." And Vanning's voice was a drone, as if it was coming out automatically while his mind was somewhere else. And in his mind he saw the black of the night all over Denver. And the woods. And then the hill. He climbed the hill. There was a field. He crossed the field. There was a stream. He stepped into the stream and the water came up to his knees and went on rising and came up to his waist.

"So he's standing there," John said. "He's pointing the gun at you—"

"I took the gun out of my pocket and showed it to him. It's hard to explain. At the time, at that exact second, I wasn't thinking of using the gun. I don't know what I was thinking. I knew he had his mind made up to kill me and I guess the whole thing was a little insane, the way I took out the gun and showed it to him. All he did was stand there and stare at the gun as if it was some new kind of gadget. I don't even remember telling myself to pull the trigger."

"When you produced that gun," Fraser said, "you must have given him the shock of his life. The way you took it out. The way you showed it to him. If you had actually drawn the gun with the intention of using it, you would have had as much chance as a fly arguing with a spider. What you did was throw him completely off balance, but even so it was a crazy thing for you to do."

"I've been doing a lot of crazy things," Vanning said, and for an instant his eyes hit Martha.

Fraser hauled deeply at his cigarette. "I think we're finally tying it up," he said, and then he looked at Vanning. "There's only one more thing, and if you can give me that, we'll have this entire business boxed and wrapped and ready to ship."

"I can't," Vanning said.

"Try."

"I've been trying. I've tried a million times. I just can't do it. I can't tell you where it is because I don't know where it is."

"Go back," Fraser said. "Take it step by step. Try to remember every detail."

And then John let out a laugh and said to Fraser, "What a panic this is. He's kidding you and you're kidding him and the two of you aren't kidding anybody. Sure, he knows where it is, but if he tells you he's a fool."

"And if he doesn't tell me," Fraser said, "he's part of that bank robbery and he goes to prison. And nothing that I say or you say or that the girl says will make any difference. Just picture it in court."

"I've done that," Vanning said. "I've done that so many times I can't stand thinking about it."

"I'll think about it for you. I'll picture it for you." There was hardness in Fraser's voice. "You're in court. They're telling you what you did. Now, here it comes. You take out the gun. You point it at Harrison—"

"I explained that."

"Explain it in court and see what happens. It's a knocked-out story, there's not an ounce of logic in it, because there's nothing to back it up. Seattle doesn't want to know from your personal troubles. Seattle wants that three hundred thousand. Listen to the way it goes. Listen—" And Fraser's voice took on a machine-gun quality, the words coming out with fire in them, coming out faster and faster, saying, "You take out the gun and you kill Harrison and you grab that satchel. You run away with it, it's three hundred thousand dollars, it's all the money in the world, it's yours, it's yours, you're not a crook and actually you didn't steal this dough, but now it's yours and you'll be damned if you're going to let it slip out of your fingers. So you take it in the woods and you dig a hole and you hide it, telling yourself when

126

you're good and ready you'll come back and pick it up—"

"But that's not true," Martha blurted.

Quiet came in like a blade as they all stared at her.

Then Fraser slowed down a little. "I don't care if it's true or not," he said. "That's what they'll say. Go argue with them. Go try and make them believe otherwise. You, John. You're on the sidelines now. Do you believe him?"

"Do I look like a moron?" John wanted to know. He grinned at Vanning. "No offense, bud. You're playing it the smart way. Stay with it. You'll be out in a few years and then it's all yours. It's a lot of jack and it'll buy you a lot of pretty things."

Vanning was staring at the floor, his head going from side to side, his hands pressing hard at his temples. "I don't know where it is. I don't, I don't know where it is."

"Think," Fraser snapped. "Think, man."

"Why don't you leave him alone?" John said. "You're carrying on like a third-rate detective."

Fraser blinked a few times. Then he smiled at John and he said, "All right, I'll leave him alone. I'm going to do better than that. I'm going to walk out, and he can have the gun."

John was a statue with big glass eyes as Fraser handed the gun to Vanning, and then the glass eyes moved slowly, following Fraser as he headed toward the door, and John said, "You must be crazy."

"Maybe I am," Fraser said. "But I trust this man. I can't help it."

"You're still not telling me anything," John said. "What's all this good-bye?"

"No good-bye." Fraser held onto the smile. "I'm only going outside to have a chat with your friends."

The glass eyes became foggy. "How do you know they're outside?"

Fraser swerved away from the door and moved across the room toward the studio couch. He let go of the smile as his eyes took in the other gun. And he said, "Even a third-rate detective would know they're outside."

Chapter Sixteen

It was strange, the way Fraser picked up the other gun. It was strange, the expression on his face as he walked out of the room. And the quiet that followed was very strange. There was a lot of ending in it. And it seemed that most of the ending was concentrated where John's gaze rested on nothing. It seemed that the ending and nothing were coming together and creating a blend. And the quiet went on. And Vanning had the gun aimed at John's face, the gun heavy in his hand, the gun seeming to gain weight with every passing second of that dismal quiet.

The quiet went on.

Finally John said, "I don't figure this. I've been trying but I can't figure it nohow."

"I could use a drink of water," Vanning said, keeping his eyes on John.

"I have some lemonade in the icebox," Martha said. She moved toward the kitchenette. She became busy with pitcher and glasses. For a few moments Vanning forgot entirely about John, and although his eyes drew a straight path between himself and John, he was seeing Martha in the kitchenette, he was seeing her walking down the street. He was seeing her in a small restaurant, and on the subway, and walking through the park. And she was alone, all the time alone. In this little place she called home, she was alone. Night after dreary night she was alone. He saw her sitting in a chair in this room, alone, and then he saw himself making his way across the stream in the black woods outside Denver, and he saw himself going through the woods, and he heard his own soundless speech as he told himself he was afraid of the satchel.

Somehow he had a glass of lemonade in his hand. He sipped at it and there was no taste. A big tree, blacker than the black of the woods, far blacker than the sky, loomed up in front of him. He was going fast, and in order to get away from the tree he had to throw his body quickly to the side. He could see part of the moon coming into view as he veered away from the tree. He couldn't see the remainder of the moon because a blotch of cloud was dangling up there. There was a flicker of white, then black, then white again, and the cloud and segment of moon came together and took on a fleshy color and the mixture molded itself into John's face. John was gulping at a glass of lemonade.

Martha was saying, "I have some scotch around here, if anyone feels like it."

"None for me," John said. "I'd better get used to the idea of no liquor."

Martha walked back and forth for no reason at all. She stood in front of the closed door that separated her little home from the rest of the house. Lightly and slowly she patted her palms against the white door, cleaned to a very white, and she said, "He's been out there a long time."

"He shouldn't have gone out alone," Vanning said.

John was shaking his head. "He shouldn't have gone out, period."

"A wife and three kids," Vanning said, the moment bursting as he remembered his first meeting with Fraser.

John frowned. "How do you know?"

Vanning didn't answer, since in a single, jumbled second he had forgotten what the question was, and besides, he was too busy dodging another tree. This was an awfully big fellow with branches going out wide, clutching frantically at the vacant sky like a punctured octopus, and there was a miniature ravine a few steps farther on, and Vanning stumbled into it, came up and out of it, got past the big rock with the sound of leather against rock a distinct recollection in his pounding brain. The leather was the satchel, so that particular tree and that particular rock didn't matter, because he still carried the satchel at that time.

Again Martha was walking back and forth. "I have a telephone here," she said. "Maybe if we made a call—"

"Better not," Vanning said. "Fraser would have made the call if he thought it was best. I guess he didn't want to take the chance of losing them. At the first sign of police they'd get scared and start running. We don't want to horn in on this. Fraser knows what he's doing."

"What's he so hungry about?" John said. "Sam and Pete don't figure now."

"Everything figures now," Vanning said. "It's Fraser's case and he wants to get all the answers tonight."

"All the answers?" John said.

"All of them."

"Except one," John said. "There's one answer he won't get, unless you lose all your brains all of a sudden. I tell you, if you hold out you'll get away with it. And suppose you do spill it, what will you get? A merit badge? Put it together and see for yourself. A cop is a cop and Fraser isn't doing anybody any favors. And if you think he doesn't have his own eye on that dough—"

"Cut it out," Vanning said. "You're way off."

"Am I?" John said. "You're new at this sort of thing. Maybe you ought to listen to an old hand. I don't claim Fraser will pull monkey business. I do claim he's given more than a single thought to the reward money, and believe me, there's bound to be some important reward money. Maybe he's not a bad guy and maybe he likes to give people a break now and then, but you can bet your sweet life Fraser comes first."

"That's why he walked out," Vanning said with weary sarcasm. "That's why he put a gun in my hand."

"Can't you see through that?"

"I see the gun in my hand. I see Fraser trying to give me a fair deal."

"And I see Fraser playing you for a sap," John said. "Sure, he puts a gun in your hand. Sure, he walks out, and you're in charge, you're the good boy of the class, old faithful in person, mister true blue, loyal to the end. And when Fraser comes back, if he does come back, you're still the good boy and you hand over the gun like a good boy. And then Fraser takes you in, and you go to prison. Like a good boy."

"What's the matter, John? Are you trying to give me ideas?"

"I'm trying to get a few angles across," John said. "If you get the point, swell. But you won't get the point. Because you like the idea of stooging for Fraser. It's easier that way. But when you see those bars in front of your face you'll remember what I told you. And you're going to hate yourself for losing out on a cute little chance that was handed to you on a silver platter."

"Save it," Vanning said. "I'm not buying anything today."

John looked at Martha and said, "Maybe you can sell it to him."

"He can do his own thinking," Martha said.

John came back to Vanning. And John's face was solemn, a rather sad note in his voice as he said, "I can see it as if it happened already. You went and got cold feet and you told them where they could find the money. So they talked to Denver and Denver laid hands on the cash and gave it back to Seattle. That made everything nice and pretty for everybody, and everybody was tickled pink. But there was one piece of business that had to be taken care of. You see, they still had to put you on trial. And it was certainly a crying shame, but even though you owned up, they still had to put you in jail because, after all, you got yourself in on the tail end of that bank job, you got your mitts on that dough and you stashed it away. It was too bad, but even though that money, every last cent of it, was back in the vault where it belonged, they still had to give you a few years. And when I say a few years I'm giving you the benefit of a great big doubt."

"It sounds very good," Vanning said. "But it doesn't mean a thing, because I don't know where that money is."

John let out a huge sigh. He turned to Martha and said, "Honest to goodness, I'm beginning to believe him." Then his head made a snapping, mechanical turn and his eyes slashed at Vanning as he said, "If you don't know where that dough is, if you really and truly don't know, then do me a little favor. Tell me one thing. You've got that gun in your hand. You've got that door in front of you. Tell me, what are you hanging around for?"

Vanning mixed a shrug with a smile as he said, "I'm trying to be a good boy."

John made a reply, but it didn't reach Vanning, because Vanning was moving through thick brush that took him downhill where there were no trees, where the moonlight made a spray of pearls on the jet velvet of moss-covered rocks, and one of the rocks became transparent, with a scene beneath its glassy substance, the scene showing

Fraser going down a stairway. Everything turned inside out and Fraser's skull became transparent, and inside Fraser's mind there was the plan to make a rear exit and take the alley and work it roundabout to Barrow Street, the anticipation of two men on the other side of the street, waiting behind a tree or behind an automobile or in an automobile or in some doorway. The realization of that was a flash containing all sorts of color, and it flashed again, and again, and then it rose and took its place on an observation post, with Fraser far below. Fraser walking alone down the dark street.

"I hate the thought of it," Vanning said. "Fraser out there alone."

John smiled like an old fox. "I knew it. Here it comes."

Vanning beckoned to Martha and said, "You take the gun."

She didn't move. She said, "I'm afraid I don't understand."

"I'm going out there," Vanning said.

"And he'll keep on going," John said. "He'll get away while the getting is good. He's not such a fool, after all." Then, as he addressed Vanning, his voice dropped a little. "While you're at it, you might as well give me a break too. I won't bother you any more. All I want to do is get myself lost."

"No go," Vanning said. "You stay here." And again he beckoned to Martha, his eyes soldered to John.

Martha stayed where she was.

Vanning's voice was almost down to a whisper. "I want you to take the gun, Martha. I want you to keep it on John. I'm going out there. You can decide for yourself. You can believe anything you want to. If you take John's word for it, I'm walking out on the whole thing and you'll never see me again."

She was breathing deeply. "And if I take your word for it?"

"I'm going out to see what I can do for Fraser."

John lifted his eyes to the ceiling as he crossed his legs and threw his hands around a knee. "That one gets four stars," he said. "That's the best I've ever heard."

Vanning bit into his lip. "I'm sorry, Martha. I hate like the devil to put you on the spot, and it's a thousand to one that

John is calling it right. I mean the way it looks on the surface. I know it's giving you a lot of worry—"

"That's not what I'm worried about." There was feminine indignation in Martha's tone. "I don't like your going out there without a gun. All you have is your two hands. What are you trying to do, show me you're a big brave man?"

"Sure," Vanning said. "And I can do somersaults, too. Here, take the gun."

Martha was moving in toward the gun, and John banged a fist into a palm and said, "I'm closing up shop. I'm way behind the times. He's actually sold her a bill of goods."

The gun in Martha's hand pointed at John's chest, and Vanning took in that picture a couple of seconds and then he stepped toward the door.

"Just keep it on him," he said. "He won't do anything. You won't do anything, will you, John? Look how nervous she is. If you let out a sneeze she'll pull the trigger."

"Is that all I have to do?" Martha said. "Pull the trigger?"

"That's all you have to do," Vanning said. He had his hand on the doorknob. "Good-bye now."

John looked at Vanning and nodded slowly, emphatically. "Good-bye is right."

The door opened, banged shut as Vanning raced down the hall, down the stairs. Now the moonlight in the black woods showed another large rock against which Vanning leaned for a few moments to catch his breath, but his hand did not touch the rock because the satchel was in there between his hand and the rock. And so that particular rock didn't matter, either. Beyond the rock, flowing in toward Vanning, there was a parade of small trees, so straight they looked as if someone had tried to start an orchard in the woods. Their amazingly well-ordered progression stood out against the rest of the woods like good soldiers in a riotous crowd. The moonlight seemed to pick them out and honor them. They passed in smart review as Vanning moved on. And then, just as Vanning reached the second-floor landing, he heard the sound of a shot.

Chapter Seventeen

It came from the street, entered the house and ripped through like an insane intruder. There was another shot. Vanning winced. He told himself to keep moving. There were more shots. The stairway rushed up at him, went past him, and he was thinking that in all probability Fraser had a little house up in Kew Gardens or someplace like that and there was a bit of grass around the place and every night when Fraser came home, Fraser's wife was there, waiting. And the children were in their beds, and Fraser would come up and kiss the children, kiss them softly, tenderly, so as not to wake them. And in the morning Fraser and the wife and the three kids would be sitting there at the breakfast table with sunlight getting through a tree out on that little lawn out there, the sunlight coming through and glowing on the toaster on the breakfast table, the chromium bright, the faces glowing, the little Fraser family.

The sunlight glowing, but then it was no longer sunlight, it was a street lamp throwing glow into the front doorway as Vanning ran out. Against the black street the glow was intense, there was some red in it, some bright red streaming curving away from a motionless form in the center of the street, the nucleus of the red a distinct blotch on the side of Sam's balding head.

That was the first thing. The second thing was the big rubber band of quiet that stretched and stretched before the next shot. When he heard the next shot, he traced the sound of it to a doorway across the street, he saw a big man moving out of the doorway, saw the big man making bold progress down the stone steps. Then he saw something moving slowly, going down at the side of a telegraph pole, knees giving way. His eyes switched back to the big man who advanced across the street, the big man pointing a gun toward the weak and sagging thing that was trying to wrap itself around the telegraph pole, trying to push the pole between itself and the advancing gun.

All of this was coming nearer, getting larger, especially the big man, who was now very big. And on the border of all this, as another shot sounded, there was sideline activity, windows opening, the sound of people, but it was part of the vague black, it was absurdly unimportant. The only thing that mattered was the big man, so terribly big now, the bigness suddenly blending with a swift turning, the motion clumsy yet definite, and all that blending with the new direction of the pointed gun, and then the blast, quickly followed by another blast from the gun now pointed at the sky because Vanning had a hold on Pete's wrist, and with his other hand he was bashing away at Pete's face with all his strength.

Pete wouldn't let go of the gun. He aimed a knee at Vanning's stomach, missed and tried again, and this time his knee made contact and Vanning fell back, doubled up, lost his balance and fell heavily on his side. And he stared at the gun, the huge, twisted face behind the gun. On the gun there was a gleaming and in the black woods outside Denver there was moonlight gleaming and then from somewhere behind the moonlight there was the sound of another gun, and Pete stood very straight just before he arched his back and dropped the revolver and followed the revolver to the street. He did some groaning, a little gurgling, and then he was all finished, crumpling in a heap over the revolver.

Vanning pulled himself up, made a dash to the telegraph pole. He took hold of Fraser and saw the pain on Fraser's face.

"How did I do?" Fraser said in a kind of gasp.

"Very nice. Where has it got you, Fraser?"

"A knee job. Hurts like hell." And all at once Fraser's eyes were very wide but not with pain. "What are you doing here?"

"It's all right," Vanning said. "She's watching him. She has the other gun on John."

"She sure has," Fraser said, grinning through the pain, his eyes going past Vanning, so that Vanning had to turn and see what it was all about. For an instant all he saw was people running out of doorways. The instant crumbled and the people faded and he saw John approaching, followed by the gun and then Martha. He felt like laughing out loud. It was a wonderful little picture. Martha looked so serious about it all, and John looked so weary, as he walked forward.

A hand touched his shoulder, and he came back to Fraser, and Fraser was saying, "You sure put yourself out for me. It's going to be tough on me, taking you in, along with our friend John."

"That's all right," Vanning said. "Don't let it bother you." He was ripping the fabric of a trouser leg, using the freed fabric to fashion a tourniquet. As he tightened the tourniquet, he heard Fraser's groan, but he went on with the tightening, then the knotting, and just as he finished the knotting he saw Martha and John standing there, and all the gaping people behind him. He saw that and yet he didn't see it, because he was staring at the black of the woods where it was all very thick and jumbled compared to the twenty yards or so of muddy clearing that separated this thick vegetation from those mathematically arranged trees.

Someone was talking, but Vanning didn't know who it was and he didn't know what was being said. Now, in this heavy foliage, he didn't have the satchel, but moments ago while going past the final tree in that strangely straight row, he had held the satchel in his hand. And his brain took a skip and a jump. The satchel was somewhere in that small clearing. Between the tree and the foliage, and closer to the foliage, and it was there, it had to be there. Somewhere in that area the satchel had to be there.

Fraser was watching him. Martha was watching him. And John. He didn't know that. He was back there in the dark woods, going toward the satchel.

And all at once a voice said, "Where? Where is it, Jimmy? Where?"

It was Martha's voice. He looked at her, and he could see the pleading in her eyes, the hope and the fear. And then he couldn't see her eyes but he could see the satchel. His eyes were shut tightly and he could see the satchel glimmering as it dropped away from him and went into a little muddy crevice about three yards away from the foliage, between the foliage and the trees.

And there it was, and it was still there, a little thing of black leather glowing in the moonlight, a little lost thing waiting for someone to come along and find it in the crevice and pick it up.

No doubt. No fear. Only the knowledge. The bursting wonderful discovery. And the wonderful realization that the woods were extremely dense and there were no paths in that vicinity and the satchel would still be there and the landmarks were convenient and specific and he could lead them to the satchel, could lead them to the very spot where the satchel lay.

His eyes lit up and he grinned at Fraser.

The detective grinned back. "You finally hit it?"

Vanning nodded. "On the button. Right on the button."

"It isn't buried, is it?"

"No," Vanning said. "It's in the open."

"You dropped it while you were running?"

Vanning nodded.

"You dropped it and kept moving," Fraser said. "That's what I was hoping you'd tell me. I'll go along in that trip to Denver. I'll back you up, even though it isn't really necessary. Any good psychiatrist could figure this without any trouble."

"Do you have it figured yourself, Fraser?"

"A hundred per cent," Fraser said. "It's what they call regressive amnesia. You identified the satchel with your killing a man. Subconsciously you forced yourself to forget the location. Something important had to happen to get you past that barrier. Now if the important something will hand over the gun she's got in her hand there—"

Martha placed the revolver in Fraser's extended hand. That made two guns on Fraser's side. The guns aimed casually in the direction of John, but John wasn't looking at the guns. He seemed far away from the whole business. He didn't even blink when he heard the sirens, although he knew they were coming toward him and toward no one else.

between her production and
we die siders dunss? dass her production
because ill never? ? only? over's? deeson
and her production is hard
1) can be? ?
2) ? that ?
3) ever
4) face full? ? ?
5) ? ? by huth